EGR
NEW OPENINGS IN

EDITORS
David Winters
Andrew Latimer

ASSISTANT
Lily Hackett

ILLUSTRATION
Catrin Morgan

DESIGN
Andrew Latimer
Jessica Kelly

PUBLISHED BY
Little Island Press

SUBSCRIPTION
£12 per issue; £20 per annum

INFO
ISBN 978-1-9998549-1-1 (ISSN 2515-2491)

CONTACT
www.littleislandpress.co.uk/egress
egress@littleislandpress.co.uk
twitter.com/EgressMag
instagram.com/egressmagazine

EGRESS / ˈiːgres / n.
1 the act of leaving a place;
emergence
2 the way of leaving;
an opening or exit

EDITORS
Attention!
6

KIMBERLY KING PARSONS
Two Fictions
8

GRANT MAIERHOFER
Everybody's Darling
18

GORDON LISH
Two Fictions
22

LAURA ELLEN JOYCE
The Art of Deer Stalking
40

ASHTON POLITANOFF
Two Fictions
46

CARRIE COOPERIDER
Unhausfrau
54

CHRISTINE SCHUTT
A Happy Rural Seat of Various View:
Lucinda's Garden
58

KATHRYN SCANLAN
Two Fictions
72

REMEMBERING HOB BROUN
i Kevin McMahon 81
ii The Lost Journal PLATES
iii Sam Lipsyte 89

DIANE WILIAMS
The Important Transport
94

EVAN LAVENDER-SMITH
Two Unknowns
98

DAVID HAYDEN
Two Fictions
108

ELEY WILLIAMS
Tether
132

LILY HACKETT
Two Fictions
142

BRIAN EVENSON
A Report on Translation
148

GREG MULCAHY
Slide
152

VERONICA SCOTT ESPOSITO
Attention & the Future of Narrative
184

SPONSORS
204

CONTRIBUTORS
212

The Editors

Attention!

'**Works of imagination excel** by their power of attracting and detaining the attention', Samuel Johnson once wrote. In a time of increasing distraction, conventional fiction can no longer detain our attention. Rather, the future belongs to those strange outliers, those writers who bend and warp the medium into bold new shapes. And so, it is with great pleasure that we present a new magazine, *Egress: New Openings in Literary Art*. Published biannually, in the spring and autumn, *Egress* will feature new fiction, essays and art, with a focus on writing unconstrained by norms of genre, language and form. This first issue showcases some of the most pioneering writers working on both sides of the Atlantic today. Some of those writers are well-known names; others remain undiscovered by the mainstream. Some are publishing their very first pieces in our pages. All, we believe, are creating literary art that demands to be looked at. Turn the page, then, and look. To quote Joseph Conrad, we aim, 'above all, to make you see'.

Editors

Kimberly King Parsons

Two Fictions

MR CORPULENT WANTS POLAROID PROOF

It's what they all want. He says, 'Can you blame me?' I say, 'I'm thirsty'. This body I have is new. Mr C. and I are both a little afraid of it. It's too much – over the top. The way it moves and swells, the sounds it makes. Let's keep the body happy. The body wants water. The body wants dick. 'You're so young,' Mr C. says, amazed. 'I'm dehydrated,' I say, to show how serious.

Mr Corpulent puts his camera down, takes the silver bucket and thunders out the door. Ice is crucial in hotel rooms. Never in your life has ice been so important.

While I'm waiting I try to picture how I look, what I am for Mr C. – me from the door he's just walked out of, me from the other bed where his camera is resting. I can't know.

People reach through their machines to connect in rooms like this one. There is a pad of stationary on the nightstand, little plastic cups wrapped in plastic. In the mirror is the body, reclining. She looks ripe. Ready. I try to match her throb but mostly I'm bored.

Fat is fine. Honestly, it's my favorite part, proof of a man who wants and wants. That's not my problem with Mr C. He's just – gentle. Big but small, he blots out nothing.

To convince me to meet him here, he took a whack at being clever. 'Which is your favorite moon of Jupiter?' he asked. 'Which is your least?' He was trying to separate himself from the rest. Who isn't? I should've been more specific. Like: I need someone to smother light and sound, to smush me and smush me until I'm condensed. A modicum, a mote. A mite? Tiny, is my point.

'My wife is sick,' is how Mr C. explained himself. These machine guys, they all have someone horizontal to blame. They have dying women or dead women. They have cheating women full of heat, eating hearts, blood running out from their smiles.

The body perks up when Mr C. booms down the hall and back to the door. The lock is the type that takes a card. He sounds slumped out there – I listen to him fumble for a green flash. He is swiping the thing through at the wrong speed.

If he can figure out how doors work it will end this way: I will beg him to be heavy and the ice will come in handy. He'll flash and flash his camera. He'll pinch his photos with fat fingers and wave them about. The body will develop into something creamy. I'll make him crop out the skull, per our agreement.

When a voice in the hall says, 'Housekeeping,' Mr C. and I freeze but the body will let out her breath and turn from us, finished. She'll stand up and pat her hair, use her thumbs to swipe the black from under her eyes.

'Now's good,' the body will say to the door. She'll pull it wide open while Mr Corpulent and I rush to tidy ourselves. The body will spin on her naked toes and walk out, past the maid clutching her tiny tubes and bars, past the cart heaped with soiled and unsoiled sheets.

Mr Corpulent and I will button and zip and the maid will blink at us, knock soft on the doorframe. We'll nod. 'Now's fine,' we'll say. She'll pick a pillow to shake out and Mr C. and I will sit together on the edge of one bed, watching as she makes up the other.

WISDOM TO KNOW THE DIFFERENCE

We were working our way through the loathsome capitals. In Topeka, a lesser tornado slurped up our lawn chairs and spit them out down the block. Our place in Des Moines was shaped like a dog bone. A perv in Little Rock slithered through our basement window and fished Jo's wet panties out of the washer. I picked up a metal baseball bat somewhere along the way. I called it our home security system and brought it into every bed with us.

Jo always found a spot as a waitress, and after she'd enchanted the management of whatever restaurant, she'd get me a job sizzling or stir-frying in the back. Nights, we'd hang our stinking uniforms off of balconies, fire escapes, or porches, depending on the setup. There's a reason people in foodwork stay up late, drinking and drugging. Your shift ends and hours later you're still sweating from those burners, amped up and pissed at whichever customer or coworker screwed you the hardest. With nothing to take the edge off, Jo and I used the TV like a narcotic. We'd sit in the blue light until one of us dropped.

Rock bottom was Cheyenne. We ended up in a motel – cheap, but more than we could afford. There were no jobs. In my drawer was a shrinking roll of cash. We drank a lot of near-beer, sagged in the gruesome middle of the country.

• • •

First was a scrap of pastel paper handed over by the desk clerk, then the little light on the phone in our room started blinking. 'One of us has a big mouth,' Jo said.

She wasn't wrong. I still kept in touch with all three of my brothers, snuck out to call them and my mom and a guy I used to play cards with. We talked small, the how are yous, how 'bout them Cowboys? Things didn't have to be as dramatic as Jo made them, cutting people out whole, inking faces like life was a goddamn yearbook. I played dumb, let her scream at me, then I'd rub her feet. We'd sit on the bed, take turns sifting through calls from her AA sponsor and my wife and kid. The sponsor and the wife left their names only or were hang-ups – sometimes somebody breathing – but the kid, he left messages.

'You coming back or are you gone, gone?' he wanted to know.

He wasn't my blood kid but try telling him that. His real father felt compelled to set mobile homes on fire, people and all, and now he was in a cell, waiting his turn to be injected to death. I never planned on being a family man – still, that psycho made me seem downright paternal, and the kid took to me right away. I'd lose whole afternoons on the floor playing with him, and it was tranquil, truly, since what he called playing was just us setting up these little fairytale animals – plastic dragons, those troll dolls with the hair – into rows and rows and rows. He seemed excited just to have me near, and he'd look at my face for praise with every piece he put down.

Now, he wondered, could he maybe come live with me? Just for a little while? He had a few bucks in his piggy bank, plans to pack some snacks, stick his thumb into traffic. It turned your heart. JoJo couldn't take it. She didn't have any kids of her own – she'd had some medical deal where they'd had to scoop everything out – but she was tender when it came to little ones, for reasons she wouldn't talk about. Her not talking meant I knew everything, more or less. Mine wasn't Jo's first homewreck, not even close, but she had designs on being honorable from now on.

One night she was facing away from me, phone to her ear, and I could tell it was one of my people pouring into her. I couldn't be sure it was the kid's chirping or my wife's nothing, but Jo worked her thumb up and down, up and down those clear little hairs on the back of her neck.

I wasn't sure why my wife kept calling. Habit, probably. It wouldn't have been fair or right for me to call her back, though I missed her too, in my way, and wanted to hear her say the things she'd always said to me. I flexed hard to change who she was in my mind, turn her into a cousin or some sweet childhood friend, somebody safe from Jo's wrath.

The last time I'd seen my wife she was laid out crying on the kitchen floor, her long, naked feet pressed against the fridge. The word 'why' burbled up from her. I never gave an answer, and maybe I should've – the truth ends every conversation – but leaving was better. I knew she'd find love with whoever came next. She laughed easy and was beautiful in that bony-faced way of women who are too tired or busy to eat much. While I listened to her heave, I stared at the kid's scribbles on the freezer. Seemed like all he could draw was gnats and flies, but like any good mama my wife stuck magnets on all he handed over.

Jo put the phone down and sniffed, kind of casual. She looked ill, clammy and blanched, and that's saying something because she's too pale of a person already, kind of borderline albino in certain light.

'Let's keep on,' she said.

Everything was up to Jo; why pretend otherwise? Besides, her AA calls were starting to bother me about as much as my family calls ate at her. She'd been deep in the chip system back home, hooked all the way into that crew.

'There is no easier, softer way,' she always said. 'Stepwork is bestwork.'

Whether that was jargon or Jo, I wasn't sure – I couldn't always tell the pure her apart from the lingo. I quit cold. Nothing makes me want to drink more than sitting around drunks, talking about not drinking. But I didn't want Jo backsliding, not out here with only me to blame, and I guess some people benefit from being miserable in a group setting.

'You need to find yourself a new buddy?' I'd ask her, careful. 'Do a check in?'

She was touchy about it, like so many things.

'Do you see a drink in my hand?' she'd hiss. 'Wanna breathalize me, Officer Fuckoff?'

Jo had our exits down to a science. She got off the bed with purpose, rushed around like we had some kind of deadline. She started packing our bag, rolling our clothes up into tight little tubes. She'd explained to me again and again how this is superior to your typical folding, for reasons of space and structure both. When she was finished, our dirty jeans and t-shirts looked like crayons in a box. This was a point of pride she made sure I appreciated.

Pussy whooped, that's what one of my brothers called me. Sprung on the squirrel. 'A girl like that flashes ass, you grab some, sure,' a different brother said. 'You don't ruin your life over it.'

Jo did the shake down, went around throwing open drawers, turning on lights and looking under furniture for things we might have forgotten. I almost put down a fiver for the maid but couldn't bring myself to, though the thought alone left me feeling kind and generous of spirit. All of this leaving is what the AA people call pulling a geographic. Trying to outrun your problems, aka switching deck chairs on the Titanic, aka running with your butt on fire. I knew this and Jo knew I knew this, but like everything else, the decision was hers.

Let's call it love – you don't deserve it, you've known all along, but then somebody as misguided and hopeless as you shows up and you think: maybe. I shouldered our bag, made it as far as the threshold when the zipper popped and spewed our shit out into the hall. It was like the thing exploded. Jo squinted at me and sucked air through her teeth. She dropped to her knees and started wadding stuff up, feeding it back in, this time without any grace.

There's more you should know about her — about how, when she was afraid or concentrating hard, she'd work a hank of that dirty-blond hair into her mouth and chew.

Grant Maierhofer

Everybody's Darling

I suppose I took to mother's unders when the end became too sure. I felt myself foraging, is what it was. I'd walk through her room, run my fingers through necklaces strung over vanity mirrors. I picked up and moved when her coughing got to me.

Growing up I'd puttered after my mother fawning. I wrote my old man off early – he walked about yawping, worked cleaning classrooms, emptying garbages at the university. Easy would've been he'd died first. This was not his way, so close to mom I'd stuck.

All I could do was pace around her place those nights choking down Salem after Salem. Her past was strewn around the living room: old records smeary with dust or globs of gum, receipts slid into their lining; T-shirts from various colleges in fading oranges and reds; empty bottles of French wine and sunglasses she'd prided since I was young.

It was several weeks after she died that I started digging through dressers. Wherever she'd lived my mother had anointed each space with ornate touches of lace and glass that made one tiptoe. On previous visits I'd kept my vulgar habits at bay. I'd hawk and spit and belch in my car while collecting her medicines. Now I no longer felt those urges. Whatever had made me want to yell and assert my living had vanished, quiet, as though never there.

People are bad, I say. That's what my mother said. Her father was, so she ran away. Ten years on, she finished school while my not-aunt Lila held an anxious whining me upon her lap, watching. Watching my mother drive in mornings well before dawn to teach, study, teach, study. Lila and my grandmother watched me and all day we'd spend in the yard with pups. I was raised amid women. Women: eyes glorious with color, hair pulled up as if in shrieking horror from the skin. I worship these women.

I am not an artist, I promise. I'm not even really suffering. Just second-guessing.

I am intruding – I am an intruder – how unsavory mother would find it. I open the drawer of a dark wood chest and I see them. A sea of pinks and whites, offwhites and yellows. Silk, lace, small blankets, warm serviettes. I pull in a pile of the laundered unders and throw them gleeing onto the bed. I don't jump backward trusting, but fall face-forward into the mass, and for the first time since she passed, fall asleep.

After weeks of whatever it is I have a troubling discussion with Sissy.

'I didn't pursue anything, Sissy. You never knew the mom I knew. Her teeth sank into you, bigger than life. All she had to do.'

'Have you talked to anybody but me since she died?'

'I've done what I can.'

I can't talk to Sissy.

The stuff we press to ourselves to feel less dead. I wear a dress. My mind is circling. I love my mother. My mother made of light and standing hand in hand with me. My mother holding me in the rain as we watch our family split. My mother in makeup, in jewelry, my mother covered with gold. My mother in undress, in between outfits. My mother tanned and polkadotted, adrift in the water. My mother and father sharing beers in the car and all of us sunburnt and tired as we wait.

The day after my mother died I found myself in a room being asked questions. I wanted to vomit. I wanted to watch my mother live and know my mother. I wanted to ask her every question about every day she'd lived and feel complete.

I pace the hardwood floors in robes and gabardine and watch the days pass. I answer my mother's mail. I touch up my makeup in my mother's mirrors and listen to my mother's records. I put on my mother's lingerie and see my blotched and balding body in mirrors my mother left strewn about and I feel at one with my mother. I smoke Salem after Salem and watch television and fill myself with foods and hear her fabrics stretch and rip at rest upon the couch and I am calm, a golden gleam in my mother's eye.

Gordon Lish

Two Fictions

JAWBONE

Not to worry. You mustn't worry. There were only two of them. Look at it this way – they were courting. That's the story for you, courting, sure. Didn't I tell you already? I think I told you already – grayish, silvery – a silvery grayishness. Please, you're blowing this all out of proportion, or is it out of all proportion? Don't blow it like that, okay? Anyway, two, I said only two – I got them both – first one, then the other. Like how else, you know? You know what I'm saying. My God, did they run. But I got them, goddamn it, the fucking filthinesses. Calm down. The thing to do is to be very calm. See the sport in it if you can. No, I don't suppose they could have gone all the way yet. Conceiving – that kind of thing. Multiplying. Right, right, I got them one at a time. They had to have already like, you know, like split. Oh, you never saw speed like this kind of speed – outrunning their glamour and racing in different directions. So that wasn't so easy for anyone who's half-asleep, so was it? Had to really hustle. Had to look sharp, you know? With my hand? God no. With the roll – with the toilet paper roll, with the stand-by roll we've been keeping at the ready in there – bam, bam – like that. Splat. Come on, I'm kidding, I'm just kidding. There was no splat. My God, there was nothing to them. No innards, not even either one of them dead with a shell. Take it easy. Look, see the achievement in it, can't you see the achievement? – it's the middle of the night, they're there in the bathroom, a pair of bugs not even coupling. Oh, Jesus, knock it off. You're being ridiculous. No, I can't show you, you don't want to see – the whole saga of it got deposited into the garbage hours ago – Jesus, just two spots not any bigger than a minute apiece. But dark ones – absolutely. Not so grayishly silveryish anymore. Well, I'm giving you the facts. Turned on the light, sat down on the toilet seat – –because me, I'm all set to read, right? Then there's this feeling of the thereness of it even before you're even seeing it. You know, the sense of there is something out of place, a difference in the format? That's the word, those are the words, take any of them – shift, format, change. Lord God, a prescience, I'm calling it, something off, a thing awry there in the given space. Bam, bam! Thank God we keep that back-up roll ready to rock and roll when it's time for the canonical shits in there – there, as they say, in the can. Oh, now quit it, will you? Will you just please relax? A couple of kibbitzers, for pity goddamn sake. Wise guys. Perps. Theatre types. They was asking for it, so I gives it to 'em. Not bam, bam – more like bam bam. Listen, honey, let's cut the crap with the commas – a case like this, operators going and getting all crazy touchy, what choice does a copper got? Oh, hey, darn – enough already, okay? All I'm doing is seeing we inject some perspective into the thing. Yes, a grayish kind of lucent effect – a little shiny, if that's what lucent means – until I slapped the fucking lucence right the fuck out of them, didn't I? No, no – you can go ahead and check the bin if you want, but I'm telling you, it'll just be blood and guts, is all. Look, I'm horsing around with you, can't you tell? Please, can't a person horse around with a person? Like lucky thing for the local citizenry someone on your side was there in there on duty on the nightbeat last night in the crapper last night. Yes, yes, they're utterly thoroughly gone to glory, you can bank on it. Blots. Dots. Snip, pip – but, you know, what's ever anywhere near snipped and pipped enough? Okay, hyphenate it all you want if that's what's sensible in a summary like this. Snip-pip in one sense, yes, positively yes – yet really in truth more like, it's all in the register of the vowels, full stop, wham! Death on a tile floor. Or is it, do you say, tiled? Anyway, a pair of grout-eaters probably. Out grazing in the dark and all star-struck as all get-out- – until they go and get themselves gob-smacked for their bother and trouble, or is it trouble and bother? No real romance in it, nothing like the duet of long-nappers the mixed metaphor the whole oratorio drawls when it drawls us. Just a yawning deficit, pests asunder. Ho-hum, we're dead. Hey, they, I said they are, them. Can't you see the symmetry in it? But you're right, all right. Incident, cognition – oops, too late, finito, it's finished, what's narrable's been narrated, not even life enough left for the vacant feeling famous on paper. Behold instead the ghastly presentiment present and as yet unaccounted for in, you know, in the tummy of your overfed insect. The weight of grout – and so on and so forth. Ugh. But we mustn't dwell on it. Weren't there only the two of them? Light, the light! – run, won't you? Quick – make for anything vertical! You bet, it's definitely curtains, but – goddammit, goddammit – is hopeless flight never not noticed – at least anyway, by anyway at least by the hopeful? Sweetheart, just don't you pay any of it any mind. It's all of it just a displacement in that format thing I've just been telling you about – it's all just a feeling in the night, right up until a roll of personal tissue probably comes into it – or maybe even some other household product. Well, fuck, bugs – I mean, what can anyone really do?

COURT OF THE KANGAROO

Let **C** equal the court, **D** the defendant, then let the rumpus begin!

C: What is your name?
D: Catherine Humble.
C: Of what crimes have you been accused?
D: Please, must I?
C: This is a properly constituted court, Miss.
D: I know, I know.
C: Do you repeat yourself in the presence of the court?
D: Please, Sir, is this disallowed?
C: Which is it that repetition bespeaks, sincerity or dissembling?
D: May I confer with counsel?
C: Has the defendant brought counsel to the court?
D: I guessed it best I had help.
C: 'Guessed' and 'best', do you toy with the court?
D: Honest, Sir, I'm just a kid from the provinces, you, Sir, know.
C: No matter, Miss – you will be tried as if you were as any other.
D: But, Sir, is that just?
C: Young person, you dare to instruct the court in what is just?
D: I only thought, Sir.
C: Thought, young person, thought is not your game, is it?

D: May it please the court, this bully is bullying me.
C: Miss, I am the court, with a capital C.
D: I see no capital C.
C: She admits it, then!
D: Sir?
C: A deficiency in seeing, a seeing deficiency!
D: Sir, I am trying to follow you.
C: Ah, then – now we are getting somewhere.
D: You're losing me, Sir. Please.
C: The court finds two counts of deficiency.
D: And these, Sir?
C: One respecting sightedness, the other brightedness.
D: I'm completely confused.
C: The court's very finding – so far.
D: May one ask the court for clarification?
C: One may.
D: Well?
C: The court awaits the question.
D: Oh ... mmm – clarification, please?
C: Miss, you needn't pretend stupidity, not to mention moral –
D: Obtuseness, Sir? All this because I shat on –
C: The author of *White Plains*.
D: But not on him, Sir. On the book.
C: You deny you commented on his customary attire?
D: Did I mention that?
C: How would you know how the plaintiff dresses himself?
D: Is he the plaintiff?
C: The plaintiff is in the court. Will you stand, Sir?

D: Is that him? For a very old Hebrew he's kind of cute.
C: Miss, do you see the man turned out as you said he was?
D: No, but he's had time to change his get-up, hasn't he?
C: If you will, Miss, the court will ask the questions.
D: Begging your pardon, Sir. All I'm doing is saying.
C: Are you indeed, Miss? And do you say with prejudice?
D: I like Jews. Are you Jew?
C: Let the court note the defendant's remark.
D: Shit, guys, a girl is getting railroaded here.
C: Do you now see Mr Lish for the first time?
D: I do.
C: You state you had not seen him before writing your review?
D: I do.
C: Then why, Miss, did your review speak to his usual attire.
D: People talk. He's been talked about.
C: Then you admit you reacted to rumor?
D: Don't people always?
C: Are reviewers paid to review a writer's clothes?
D: If they're hip, they are.
C: How much were you paid?
D: Not talking, buster. Professional secret.
C: You are a professional book reviewer?
D: You got it. That's me.
C: You took on Mr Lish's book in the *Times Literary Supplement*?

D: I did.
C: Did you discuss the matter with a senior person there?
D: The guy probably, what do you say, did with me.
C: Did this senior person seek to influence your opinion?
D: Didn't have to. Everybody knows this bozo's a crum.
C: So you approached the task from a parti pris position?
D: How's that?
C: Let us say not impartially.
D: Buddy, you sure can say that.
C: Is the court correct in assuming this owes –
D: I don't owe nobody nothing. What's the bloke bleeding about?
C: Do I call you Doctor Humble?
D: Yeah, I got me a doctorate, what's it to you?
C: You enjoy the prestige of a doctoral degree?
D: Fucking A, man.
C: Did your scholia bear on work by a Raymond Carver?
D: It did.
C: Did you, in your work, Miss, take note of the plaintiff's –
D: Yeah, yeah, that cocksucker sitting right there, he murdered –
C: Mr Carver's writings, do you say?
D: Fucking right, I say. Bitching kike done Carver real wrong!

C: How so, would you say.
D: Fucking around with the guy's shit. My God, you guys crazy?
C: The court asks how you came to know of Mr Carver's writings?
D: Everybody knows about them. They're world-famous.
C: And as a literary scholar, you read them.
D: You bet your ass I did. Slayed me. Like, wow, dynamite.
C: But what you read, was that not what Lish altered?
D: Yeah, but, fuck, I didn't know no better.
C: But there was a feeling bestirred in you. Various feelings.
D: Well, yeah. Near wet me knickers more than once, okay?
C: So the court must conclude that it was –
D: Oh, shit, sure – I see where you're going with this.
C: Miss, where is it, you say, the court is going with this?
D: Fuck, Pops, you're trying to tie me up in – oh, I got you, Dad.
C: Quite right. There can be no doubt you do.
D: Hey, isn't this what they call a kangaroo court?
C: And what of it? Have you any idea what a real court would –
D: Do to me? Fuck that, man. Everybody dumps on Lish.
C: Would you go so far as to say it's a profit stream?
D: So?

C: Have you heard the expression share and share alike?
D: You're telling me the rat would settle for a cut?
C: Fair is fair, Miss. How much did the *TLS* pay you?
D: Ah, come on, Daddykins, a girl's got to get by, okay?
C: Suppose Mr Lish would agree to redo your writing?
D: Me? Mine? He'd do that?
C: Could be worth quite a pretty penny. What do you say?
D: You're saying I could email my shit to him in the US.
C: That sound tempting to you?
D: And he'd fix it the way he fixed Carver?
C: Shall the court tell you how rich Lish made Carver?
D: That bugger there would do that for me?
C: The court is prepared to cite the widow's annual income.
D: Them royalties she got? Movie money and all that shit?
C: Plus the fame, the prestige, the honors, history itself.
D: I'd be like a rumor writ large – all to myself.
C: You could quit your, is seedy the word, employment?
D: Oh, God, do I want do get gone from that asswipe outfit!
C: And your workshoppers.
D: Sweaty clot of hopeless yobs, Christ Jaysus.

C: Think of the conferences, the convocations – the retreats.
D: Yeah, dick galore at them things. And if I liked the ladies –
C: Lish'd make you the lead attraction, the top draw.
D: Wouldn't have to look up words no more.
C: Exactly, Miss. Lish's 'stochastic' his 'chthonic', you –
D: I could forget all about that crap like that.
C; Not a bad deal, wouldn't you say?
D: Pretty sweet all around, you know? But the *TLS* folks, they'd–
C: They'd what? Punish you for looking out for number one?
D: Like me first debut thing comes out, they'd be laying for me.
C: But why? The court encourages you to say why.
D: A girl'd be on their shitlist, like Lish is on everybody's.
C: Not impossibly.
D: They'd set me up. Rig it against me. Bring in a hit-man.
C: Oh, Catherine, darling, surely you've heard it said that –
D: What goes around comes around? I have, I have.
C: Did you not take this into consideration when you feathered –
D: Me nest? No, not anything adequately, I guess.
C: You are aware you misread Lish's title?
D: I did?

C: Did you not check the review before you handed it in?
D: They got them checkers there, fancy types. La-di-dah interns like.
C: A lazy rotten lot, Cathy. A player gets played. Look sharp.
D: I said he said 'witherings' when it was 'witherlings', did I?
C: You did, darling. Pilloried him for it, too, now didn't you?
D: Oh, my. I was so nervous and all – him such a bigshot.
C: Child, you were well out of your depth.
D: Ach, but it was them boyos which made me.
C: Took you for a greenie, they did. So sorry, lass.
D: I heard a riot of letters come in. Hot ones. People pissed.
C: Stepped in it, didn't you, sweet thing?
D: Not to take the money if you can't do the time.
C: Is that what they say?
D: Made a mess of it, haven't I?
C: Do you know a person name of Crackel, then?
D: She after me, too?
C: Not to fear, Ms Umble, not to fear. Very gentle, she is.
D: Is she really? And who would she be?
C: A friend of the court, you might say.
D: An associate of this Lish of yours, then?
C: In a manner of speaking, yes.
D: So? Your point, Sir?

C: Dr Umble, you go on back home. The court will sort Lish out.
D: Must've hurt the man, the bit about the big hat and all.
C: Oh, no need to take on. He loved you for your haplessness.
D: A big galoot with a great big heart, is he? That's grand.
C: Crackel will be your go-between. She'll call on you.
D: Collect me manuscripts? Me papers and all that?
C: Right you are. Enid's the name. She'll liaise with Lish.
D: How's that?
C: Hook the two of you up.
D: He won't be asking for me to do anything funny, now.
C: Just wait for Enid, dear child – she'll come to your door.
D: Is it all right if we do our business at the college?
C: It would be risking discovery, girl. We'll want the lid on.
D: Right, we will, will we not?
C: Very nicely turned, Cath – dashedly nice.
D: You think so, do ya? I turnt it meself.
C: Lovely is as lovely does.
D: See how it's already taking, Mister, do ya?
C: I do.
D: So we square, then?
C: Couldn't be more geometric, if I say do so myself.

D: But ya don't, do ya?

C: Are you telling me something, Umble? What is it, what?

D: What with the elder party pulling the strings, you know.

C: Is there something wrong with that, do you think?

D: I'm just saying.

C: Sure, you are – but picture the life to come. Time to live!

D: 'Tis time, ain't it? Still, it feels passing strange.

C: Like Raymond must have felt, do you suppose?

D: Dunno. If he had a heart.

C: Ach, child, you said it in the review – his beating heart.

D: But then there's the soul, God knows.

C: Isn't there just!

D: Oh, sure, pick on a dead man. There's no end to this lark.

C: Not deceased by half, child. Lish's animated him – for keeps.

D: It's all so confusing. I'm not up to heady shit like this.

C: And wasn't it clear to all in the first place?

D: How's a newbie expected to handle it? What's the answer?

C: Doc U., Doc H. – leave it all to that injured yob sitting there.

D: That bugger? He's looking to me mighty pleased with his self.

C: He is, he is! – sure enough. Talking for all, talking for you.

D: It's a fact. I can see it now.
C: Hear it, you mean. Can you, dearness? Imagine it, then.
D: I imagine? Who imagines? I just keep me ear to the ground.
C: Of course you do. How does it feel as to what you hear?
D: It feels bloody awful. Powerless and all.
C: He did it to Raysie, you did it to him.
D: You're saying we're all colonizers, cannibals, ghouls, cunts?
C: Cath, baby, I am – yet what that cunt did, 'twas prayer.
D: You're saying this because he's making you say it.
C: Doc, Doc – think about it, think! Didn't he make you?
D: Your point is nobody's got anything without everybody?
C: Me, I'd say instead 'no one' and 'everyone'.
D: Fuck, pal, this is scary.
C: Dr Catherine Humble, may one speak as the court?
D: Out with it, creep. Talk!
C: Little lady, scary you say?
D: You got it, Captain – freaky is as freaky does.
C: Child, child, bethink yourself – resay your harsh sayage.
D: No can do, yer 'oner, that there's the very the drift of it.
C: There's an expression.

D: I'm waitin', I'm waitin'. We're all of us is waitin'.
C: It goes like this.
D: All ears, bustifer – shoot!
C: You do not know the half of it.
D: Sounds pretty Jew to me, Cap.
C: Chickie baby, what am I, an impersonator?
D: Don't you mean furrier?
C: Righto, girlio – what am I, a furrier?
D: Yeah, but the fuck is making me be someone I'm not!
C: Isn't this the very thing you did to him?
D: I was writing a review of his book.
C: No, you were declaring him to be a person he isn't.
D: Who says he's not?
C: You reviewed your construct, and then pissed on it.
D: I did my job.
C: You followed orders. You took hold of an axe.
D: It's not fair. He's taking advantage, profiteering.
C: It's what makes the world go 'round.
D: I was taught it's love which does.
C: You think he doesn't love? The slob, he loves too much.
D: Loves himself too much, is what the cunt loves.
C: Pity the gob who don't. But it's the words he's mad for.
D: Is he, then? Sick, he is. Mad, all right.
C: Gone bonkers for peeking under the skirts of words.

D: Diseased. A perv for all seasons.
C: You might say.
D: Blimy, I do say.
C: See there, he give you that. Look what he's doing to me.
D: Dirty old thing ought be stopped. It's the clink for him.
C: It's that poor devil you gigged like a toad. For shame!
D: Bullshit, you fink! He's got all of you all balled up.
C: True, true, all too true. But listen, young thing.
D: Okay, I'm listening. What, what? This better be good.
C: We're showing today a very nice buy on hand-dyed ermine.
D: You people! Who can win with you people?
C: Such a genius at last! From her lips please to God's ears.

Laura Ellen Joyce

The Art of Deer Stalking

The beautiful motions of the deer, his picturesque and noble appearance, his sagacity, and the skilful generalship, which can alone ensure success in the pursuit of him, keep the mind in a constant state of pleasurable excitement.
William Scrope, *The Art of Deer Stalking*, 1838

Where we now stood had once been electrified. The deer had not been safe then, not outside their enclosure. The searing hide, the gape of flesh, the hot steam rising from their viscera, came back to us in a sick gulp as we saw the prints in the snow: his thick, heavy boots stalking a pattern of skimming hooves.

We had not been back for ten years, not since the destruction of the fences. Now, rhododendrons had taken hold. A deceptive canopy of fresh rose and lilac petals disguised the decaying mulch of dead plants, the weeds entwining fallen branches and twisted roots. Our journey had been treacherous, made more difficult in the snow.

At dusk, we had finally arrived at the burned part of the forest, where nothing grew. He still held his meets here, where there was nowhere for the deer to hide. The annihilated landscape was glacial and empty. Except for the two sets of tracks.

The red doe, pregnant and heavier than usual, had outrun him, even in this unseasonably heavy drift, because he had been drunk for some days now, drunk and raging and miserable. And with nothing but pity for his own predicament. His prints skewed left as the doe's ran true north, her skittering across the icy waste no match for his bloated, lumbering trudge.

We were silent as we followed the route she had laid out for us. We were sharp, sober, focussed. Each of us held something useful: a spade; a large torch; a litre of water; a hunting knife. Our boots were laced tightly and our socks neatly tucked into the bands of our trousers. We had thermal underwear and woollen hats and insulated gloves. We had flasks of strong coffee and cereal bars, nips of whiskey in flasks in our sensible padded jackets. We were prepared for the long haul. To stake out our prey.

For the proper adherence to ritual we had shaved our hair ultra-close, and smeared on a square of silver zinc that morning. We shone in the pale light, our glittering scalps catching the last rays of sun. Back then, he didn't permit us to cover our heads with scarves or hats in case it was discovered that we had secretly been growing our hair. Having long hair was a sign of disobedience, a way for us to integrate more easily if we managed to escape.

The light was diminishing, as it does suddenly in early November, in the first brutal days after the clocks change. It was almost four and the clear, bright sunlight had ebbed to twilight and the blue sheen on the snow-covered woodland was made only gloomier by torchlight. It was time to break, have coffee, wait for night to fall hard so the torchlight would again be useful. There was no rush, no urgency. Speed was less important than persistence, now. Surprising him would be easy, carrying out the attack with efficiency, and discretion, but only if we worked as one, with no hysteria, no emotion, no remorse.

We handed round coffee and whiskey but no one wanted food. There was a thrill of anxiety in the group, even though we were prepared for the task, though we knew we wouldn't be leaving the woods without him. Without discussion, we made a pact of silence; conversation might unbalance us, might force us to retrace our logic, our decision of the day before. There was no other way to punish the man we all had cause to hate, no way to protect the vulnerable from his greedy, sloppy attacks. Nothing less than what we had planned would do. We replaced the lids on hip flasks, screwed thermoses shut. Warmed, stimulated, refocussed, we were ready to continue tracking his lolloping progress again.

One of us held the torch high; a flat swathe of light carpeted the crunchy white earth and lit our procession. We were cold but the snow was still dry, clean, powdery and not yet the grey sludge that would persist for the next week or so, blurring the woodland with dirt, fallen leaves, and refrozen hard earth, so treacherous underfoot for the deer. The autumn stalking meets would be cancelled for a few days, and certainly long enough to put some distance between our plan and any potential accidental discovery. No one but him would be arrogant and stupid enough to come out in these conditions, trying to outsmart these beautiful, intelligent animals. Our disgust was sharpened.

The deer tracks were long gone, but his brutal prints were bedded deeper and deeper in the crystalline snow. He was near. Very near. A hut made from corrugated tin was visible in the light of the torch. This sorry location was his base of affairs, his office. We had discovered, at the time of the destruction of the fences, drawers amateurishly padlocked in there, full of the kind of material a man like that might be expected to have. Material that would make any one of us sick if we were to think properly, even for a moment, about what he hid in his desk drawers, below his locked gun cabinets, his trophies, and his books. We pressed on.

We thought he must have seen us then, seen the light, heard the soft shuffle of boots on snow, the slow movement of a mob in the dead of the woods, in the dark, while he was alone. We hoped he was scared, we hoped he was anticipating the worst.

We were there. We were ready.

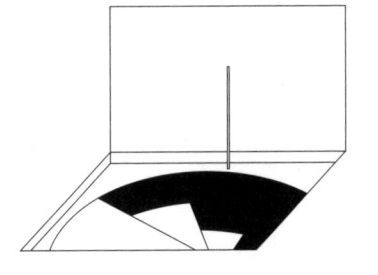

Ashton Politanoff

Two Fictions

I LIKE IT

He took his date to a tucked-away spot, a place where you could lay out unseen. He took his date up into the hills.

The parking lot near the school was full so they parked on the road by the cliff-side church. A blonde stooped down to pick mushrooms off her lawn. When she was done, she dumped the handful into her trash. Everything here was stucco and clay-tile.

Under an arm, they each carried a board barefoot to the paved road that led down to the sandy beach. When the road turned to dirt, a lizard darted out of its hole into some shrubs. They had a view of the bay now, the whole beach dotted with umbrellas and bathing suits of different color, the ocean smooth and blinding. He pointed towards the peninsula – they were getting away from all this.

Near the shoreline where the sand was hard and wet, she clamped off the waterproof bag and handed it to him. He pushed his board into the water and placed the bag on the nose. Then, prone and paddling, he aimed for the point. To their left was the coast, fishermen perched with poles.

Lots of fish, one of them hollered.

He too had promised her dolphins, whales, crabs, but they didn't see much – just a school of skittish smelt.

On the way, they cruised by a private pool built into the cliff. Bathers sat behind the glass, facing them, the sea. He stroked deeper and harder, paddling faster.

As they neared the rocks, the water cleared and filled with neon sea grass. The cliff face had tufts of brush.

Here, he said, as tiny waves pushed them closer to a bald spot. When it was shallow enough, he slipped off his board and grabbed the bag. He flipped the board over so the fin wouldn't scrape against rock. Bearing his weight on the board, he lightly stepped until he was ankle deep. Then he placed the bag on a boulder.

When he was out of the water safely, he stuck out his hand.

We made it, he said, smiling, but she did not take it. She got out on her own.

They settled on higher ground where crashing waves had smoothed things out. The tide was low enough still – it hadn't turned yet. She snapped the striped beach towel flat and sat down. A seagull hopped off a part-submerged rock as a wave passed over it, then landed back on. Among the dry and smelly stones below them, roaches scattered and hid.

Gross, she said, drawing her legs closer. It's stinky here, she said. She grabbed the can of sunscreen and sprayed it around her, not on her. She was trying to freshen the air.

No one can see us, he said. This is a tucked-away spot.

He was still standing. He removed his shorts, scratched his balls. Then, he reached down for the jar of pickles. The breeze felt good on his member and he let loose a loud one.

I like it, he said, eating the pickles one by one. Then, he tilted the jar into his mouth and slurped.

Come on, he said, get naked – but when he looked down, she was no longer there. She was skipping away boulder to boulder, her hair wild. The tide was starting to rise, but he didn't plan on going anywhere.

When he started to pee, his steady stream leaned a little to the left, striking the top of his foot.

DANCE

After the yelling, his wife came running. He hadn't heard any kind of splatter. But when he looked at his son in the Jumperoo, his son's hopping feet, he saw the green chunky smear covering several panels of the wood flooring. One of his bare feet was slipping and sliding in it, caked around and between his toes. Down it had come, bursting through the side of his diaper and down one leg onto the floor.

What's wrong? His wife said, eyeing their baby, wide-eyed and innocent in his jumper.

Look at his feet! he said. Look!

I'll look after this one, he said to his wife, but she didn't hear, already looking, crouching, assessing, too close for comfort.

I'll oversee things, he said, lying slightly propped on the sectional.

. . .

Upstairs, he removed the pad from the table and brought it down. He handed it to his wife. Handed her a bag of wipes, too, their last one. He opened the front door all the way. There wasn't a breeze, just hot heavy air, but he kept it open anyways. Flies began to buzz in. His wife lifted out the child to reveal the soiled orange seat of the jumper. The distressed wood was greasy with it, some of it settled into the cracks – the smell just hung there. He started to gag.

Really? his wife said, as she wiped down the baby's feet and legs with a wet wipe.

I'll get a bag, he said, heading for the kitchen.

We're out of bags, he yelled. No answer.

Back in the living room, his wife was removing the diaper slowly and he had to turn away. Flies covered the ground.

I'm going on a bag run, he said, heading for an exit.

Wipes too, she said.

In the garage, he turned the engine on and rotated the AC dial to the max. He kicked back, sat and stared through the windshield at the things they had stored: a sheet of split-face from the bathroom remodel, dirty t-shirts now used as rags when he washed the cars. Baseball trophies and banker boxes filled with his childhood belongings, collectibles like stamps and trading cards. Surfboards and tennis racquets, camp chairs and beach cruisers. He could see it all so clearly.

He parked underground, all the way in the back and called his wife from the car.

I still feel sick, he said when she answered, but then the call quickly disconnected.

Inside, he pushed the red cart down the aisles. He didn't need the cart, but he liked having something to hold onto. He couldn't find the bags on his own, so he asked someone for help. They directed him all the way to the back.

There were bags there, strong, dependable.

Walking past the bags, the wipes, he did not see the yellow tent-like caution sign propped in the middle of the baby section: *wet floor*. He slid forward, then back in his flip flops, a kind of dance against his will.

For a moment, it looked like he might not fall.

Carrie Cooperider

Unhausfrau

I forget how I got here. Doesn't matter. Stuff doesn't look too familiar, so maybe I did a drunken B & E – both the B and E of it caught on camera, no doubt, along with some girlish capering – then looks like I passed out, crushing this negative face-shape and those twin lagoons a heartbeat below it deep into the deep, deep carpet.

Witness there, raking aslope the hilly nap, the ruthless sunlight accuse me with shadows I can't explain. Pour some plaster in the voids like they do in Pompeii, won't you, and calculate the forensics? Or muff up the evidence; whatever you think is best. I trust you – we're in this together.

Then, let's see – by the time the front page and the crumpets and the cappuccino and I all came around the next morning I would have been trapped, probably; rendered breathlessly agasp by the lifestyle the place is smoggy with. That's one guess. You've got a better one, let me know. I'm not going anywhere.

Or, wait: maybe I was just born here and never left. That cocktail glass is blurred at its rim with, I believe, a crust of skin and lipstick in Mother's preferred shade, and the scent haunting the corners of the room is Father's eau de toilette, is it not?

Whatever. It's all a crapshoot.

Sorry, I do beg your pardon – was I blocking the view?

Yes, yes, yes, *of course* I belong to the garden club.

Don't be daft. How else the manure on my wellies, the lunacy of crud beneath my manicured paws? By the way, saw a big snake in the perennial bed last week – but I don't want to talk about it. In fact, there's not much to say about any of this liminality I find myself spilling through: thresholds, doors, windows, hallways, stairs – the inside creeps in and I seep out and all I can do is stare back at that dreadful Peeping Tomasina with my same sad haircut and stiff upper lip being held stark raving captive between the double-paned glass, stare her down so she knows I see her flattening the pachysandra.

I don't know what she thinks *she's* looking at.

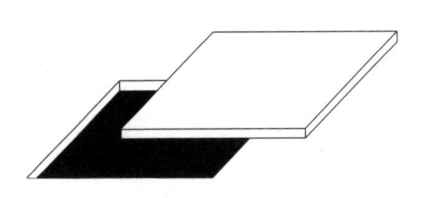

Christine Schutt

*A Happy Rural Seat of Various View:
Lucinda's Garden*

(Originally published in NOON, 2004)

They met Gordon Brisk on a Friday the thirteenth at the Clam Box in Brooklin. They pooh-poohed the ominous signs. The milky stew they ate was cold – so what? They were happy. They were at sea; they were at the mess, cork-skinned roughs in rummy spirits, dumb, loud, happy. And they really didn't have so much to say to each other. They were only a few months married and agreed on everything, and for the moment nearly everything they did – where and how they lived – was cheap or free. They expected gifts at every turn and got them.

So it was at the Clam Box on a Friday night – lime pits along the rim of the glass, Pie feeling puckered – when Gordon Brisk introduced himself as a friend of Aunt Lucinda's from a long time ago. Nick said he had seen Gordon's paintings, of course. And Gordon said, 'I'm not surprised'. Gordon told a story that included Aunt Lucinda when she was their age. There were matches in it and another young woman who almost died. Aunt Lucinda in the story was the same – all love, love, love and this time for Gordon – and as for Gordon himself? He held up his hands. His hands had been on fire. He said, 'Just look at these fuckers,' and they did. They looked and looked. The hands should have scared them, but they were drunk and sunburned and happy. They were glad, they insisted, glad to have met him. 'Our first famous person,' Pie said after the after-dinner drinks when she and Nick were in the Crosley driving home.

Pie was driving, too fast; she was saying how she loved those amber-colored, oversweet drinks, the ones with a floating orange slice and a cherry. She had had too many, so was it any surprise she hit something? She hit something large and dark, but fatally hesitant. The Crosley, a gardener's minicar, had no business on a public road, but Pie had wanted to drive it. The Crosley was a toy, yet whatever Pie hit hobbled into the woods, dragging its broken parts.

Home again and in their beds, Pie and Nick took aspirin and turned away from each other and slept. Next morning – frictive love – and then as usual in the garden, Aunt Lucinda's garden, the famous one, a spilling-over, often photographed, seacoast garden. The garden was how they lived for free. They were the caretakers of an estate called The Cottage. Some cottage! Why would Aunt Lucinda leave this paradise, they asked, but she had told them. His name was Bruno and his wealth exceeded hers. The villa he owned in Tuscany was staffed. 'Everything there is arranged for my pleasure,' so Aunt Lucinda said.

Gordon had said, 'Scant pleasure.' He had said, 'I'll tell you pleasure. The killing kind.' And then to almost everyone at the Clam Box bar, he described his wife: shoeblack hair and pointy parts. That cunt was the source of the fire, or so he had said at the Clam Box. 'I was fucking around' was what Gordon had said, 'but who wouldn't?'

They were untested, Pie and Nick. They were newly everything; and now here they were caretakers for a summer before the rest of life began, and on this morning, as on so many mornings, the cloudless sky grew blue, then bluer. White chips of birds passed fast overhead, and the water was bright; they looked too long at its ceaseless signals and at noon they zombied to it. They let the waves assault them and knock them back to shore. Sand caught in all the cracked places, and it felt good to take off their suits and finger it out. Up the beach they lay directly on the sand; they dozed, they woke, they brushed themselves off. They wanted nothing. They were dry and their suits were dry and, for a moment, warm against them, and they walked to the shore, walked along the shore and then into the water. They knew the water all over again. So went the afternoon in light – no clouds – whereas indoors was dark.

It was dark, but they ran through the mudroom toward the phone. They ran, and then they missed it. Who cared? They had the late afternoon before them.

They tended the garden. Nick and Pie, they watered the deep beds; they flourished arcs; they beaded hooded plants and cupped plants and frangible rues. They washed paths. The wet rock walls turned into gems. What a place this was! How could Aunt Lucinda's Bruno match it? Of course, the sunsets could be overlong if all they did was watch them, but they were distracted. The hot showers felt coarse against their sunburned skin and the lotion was cold. They put on pastel colors and saw their eyes in the mirror – another blue!

Another summer dusk, stunned by the sun's garish setting, they stood close to the grill and the radio's news. They were in love and could listen, horrified but untouched, to whatever the newscaster had to say. But the flamboyant infanticide accomplished with duct tape was too much. It had happened just north of them in the next and poorest county.

'Turn that off!' Nick said, and Pie did.

For them, nothing more serious than the dark they finally sat in with plates on their laps and at their feet melted drinks that looked dirty.

• • •

'Death: will it be sudden and will we be smiling? Will we know ourselves and the life we have lived?'

'Don't even think such things!'

But Pie did, and Nick did, too.

He said, 'Think of something else,' and Pie came up with Gordon.

Gordon at the Clam Box. His high color and his scribbled hair. The way he startled whenever they had swayed closer. Was he afraid he might be touched? But there were all those women. An actress they had heard of. A lot of other men's wives. Aunt Lucinda. 'A beauty,' was what he said of her. Cornelia Shelbey had been a girlfriend, too, until the Count swooped down. A prick, the Count. Cornelia Shelbey was a cunt.

'What are we?' they had asked.

'Conceited!'

• • •

Nevertheless, Gordon called them. The picnic was his idea. Mid-morning and already hot; the coast, a scoured metal, stung their eyes. Even as they drove against the wind, they felt the heat. There was no shade for a picnic. The tablecloth, held down with rocks, blew away. The champagne crinkled. The food they ate was salty or dry: no tastes to speak of. Nick wanted peanut butter and jelly on pink, damp bread. Instead here were cresses and colored crisps. Then the champagne began. Pie swallowed too much of an egg too fast and it hurt her throat.

Gordon said of Aunt Lucinda's Bruno, 'The man's a fool. He knows nothing about art, but he lets people play with his money.' Gordon picked at the knees of his loose khaki pants and what he found he flicked away into the sea grass. He asked, 'How do you play with yours?'

They told him just how little they had.

'Too bad!' he said. 'Poor you.'

Pie washed her sticky hands in the cooler's melting ice. Gordon yawned. Then they all three pushed the picnic back into the basket, didn't bother to fold the tablecloth, drove home.

• • •

A storm the next day; the power thunked out. Nick and Pie still had headaches from the picnic – too much champagne and whatever they had drunk afterward – so they took more aspirin. They napped; they looked at the sky; they shared a joint, and they knocked around in bed and felt rubbed and eased when they were finished. It was quiet in The Cottage except for the sound of the rain. They talked about money until they made themselves thirsty. Downstairs on the porch they saw Gordon in the garden under the tent of a golf umbrella.

Gordon said he'd walked all the way from the village to them, walked in the rain to get sober. 'Last night,' he said sadly. He shut the umbrella and sat on the porch with his head in his ruined hands.

• • •

So they lit the fat joint rolled against the threat of all-day rain, and Gordon was glad of it. 'Yes,' he said and inhaled deeply and exhaled in a noisy way, seeming satisfied, which was how they felt, too. Forgotten were the woozy picnic and the problems of money. After all, Nick and Pie were a handsome couple, young and loved. Aunt Lucinda was rich even if they weren't. Hundreds of people had come to their wedding, and now they were caretakers for a scenic estate called The Cottage. The Cottage on Morgan Bay. For them the sky cleared and the sun came out and the garden began to sizzle. Gordon stayed on. He watched the happy couple, swatted by the waves: how they exhausted themselves until he was exhausted, too, and he slept. They all slept. They slept through the white hours of afternoon when the light was less complex. When they woke, the sand was peachy colored, and the sky was pretty. Gordon said he wanted to do something, but what? Why didn't they have any money!

They had the Crosley. 'Fun,' Pie said.

'Some fun,' Nick said. 'You killed some kind of animal in that toy.'

Pie said, 'I could bike to Gary's and see if he has any clams. We could have a clambake.'

'Down here? After five? It's damp and cold and there's not as much beach.'

'You come up with something why don't you.'

'The lotion's hot. It can't feel good,' Gordon said, but Pie said he was wrong.

'I'm so sunburned anything against my skin feels cool,' she said.

Gordon wiped his hands on her breasts. He said, 'Lovely.' He said, 'Maybe you'll think of something to do. I'll call you.'

A line they had heard before – had used themselves. I'll call you augured disappointment.

· · ·

Nick's handsome face was crinkled. 'What the fuck was that all about?'

'What's this?' Pie asked.

'You're more ambitious than I am' was what Nick finally said.

A cup of soup was dinner; the radio, left off.

'Find some music,' Pie said and left Nick to wander

through The Cottage. She swatted Aunt Lucinda's clothes until she found his idea of ambition: Valentino tap pants, and she tapped downstairs to nobody's music but her quavery own.

'Look at you,' he said.

. . .

On the beach, they agreed, their daydreaming was sometimes dangerous. The memory of Gordon's misanthropic breath against their faces came in gusts.

'Jesus,' Pie said, remembering.

'What?'

The hollows of her body, especially at her hips, were exciting to them both, and they smiled to see the sand running out of Nick's hand and into the ditched place between her hips.

'Jesus,' Pie said.

'I was thinking I would lick.'

. . .

Back to the garden, to the doused and swabbed, every morning, afternoon. Nick staked the droopers and Pie cut back. The heavy-headed mock orange, now past, Pie hacked at and hacked at until the shorn shrub looked embarrassed.

'Poor thing,' Nick said.

And Pie laughed. 'I've turned the grandpa of the front walk into a kid.'

Pie, a long girl, wobbly in heeled shoes, bow-legged, shifty – bored, perhaps – but friendly, quick to laugh, on any errand making an impression. Nick left her on the village green the next afternoon, a lean girl in a ruffled bib. What was she wearing exactly? Something skimpy, faded, pink. She wore braids (again) or that was how Nick remembered her when he described to the police Elizabeth Lathem Day – Pie was her father's invention. A girl, a pretty speck, a part of summer and passing through it.

She was. Pie was a white blond, a blond everywhere – it made Nick hard to think of her. She had close blond fur between her legs. He liked to comb it with his fingers, pull a little bit. Fuck.

. . .

'Where the hell is she?' Nick couldn't help himself. 'Missing persons – really?'

Lucinda said there was no family precedent; no one was mad that she knew of.

'Don't think we weren't getting along. Quite the opposite.'

. . .

Dogs off leashes snuffed in the woods. Heavy yellow and black dogs, their rheumy eyes mournful, their hard tails always looked wet and whapped against the shrubs. Once the dogs barked; Nick heard though they were out of sight. They had found something dead and offensive – not her, not Pie – thank God! Although after the dogs, the reports, the calls, the case grew fainter.

• • •

Also, also, Nick was drinking. He was forgetting he had this job. He found himself standing in front of open broom closets and cabinets, in front of the dishwasher and sinks. Sometimes his hands were wet.

• • •

Watering; he finished watering the wilted patches, then sat on the porch and worried his roughed-up hands, cut and dirty and uncared for, ugly as roots and clumsy. Hard even to phone, to push the buttons accurately, but he did and to his surprise Gordon Brisk answered, and said, 'I'm only just home but I've heard. I'm sorry.'

And that was that.

What was this guy all about was what Nick wanted to know. 'Tell me,' Nick said to Lucinda. Addresses, historic districts, the watch he wore, his antique truck, Gordon's conversation was an orange pricked with cloves – an aromatic keepsake of Episcopal Christmases – so it came as a surprise when he said he was a Jew. A Jew?

'You've not seen a lot of the world, Nick.'

True, he hadn't. He had married young.

But Nick did not want to travel: he wanted to stay at The Cottage at least until spring, maybe through another summer. Who knew? Pie might come back.

• • •

Why would Gordon say more? Nick and Pie hadn't seen him since – when? That hot, flashy day Brisk discovered they only looked rich; they had money enough to get by. But how much was that? How much did it cost to get by pleasantly?

They were young, newly married. The most expensive things they bought were medicinal, recreational.

• • •

'You have no idea how happy we have been here,' Nick said. This was the truth uttered later, after whatever had passed for dinner, after the bath that made him sweat, the third or fourth Scotch. 'We were really, really happy.'

The mothers and fathers – on both sides – made visits. They remarked on the garden and the ocean; they said no one would leave such a place voluntarily. So Nick stayed on at The Cottage. He watched the seasons redden then blue then brittle and brown the plants. The decline could be beautiful, but Nick's hands, ungloved, grew grotesque. A fungus buckled and yellowed his thumbnail. His hands, all rose-nicks and dirt, reminded him of Gordon's hands. Gordon talking about something to do with love, saying they had no idea, speaking in his seer voice, the old, pocked, vacant voice, prophesying horrors they could not imagine.

Not us. Pie thought and Nick thought, too; weren't they always harmonious after Gordon left? They said, 'We're lucky.' Together: 'We are.'

. . .

'You have no idea,' Gordon had said another day on the beach. He had said to Nick, 'Someday your mouth will bleed in your sleep, and her cunt, too, will stain whatever it touches.'

'Love?'

Gordon in the buff on the beach that time, pulling at the bunched part between his legs, lifting up a purse of excitable skin. The black-haired, peaky creature known as his wife had been a cunt. Gordon had said, 'I was on my way home when I saw the smoke. Up in smoke! My wife and some of my paintings.' Gordon had asked, 'You know what I tried to save, don't you?'

Nick had suspected it was not his wife.

But what was Nick doing to find his?

Why was it Gordon that Nick thought so much about when Gordon had shut up his house and gone somewhere south, southwest?

. . .

Oh, the summer! The summer felt next door despite the cold. Nick talked to anybody. He shut the place up. He was there after last call, at the bar, saying his goodbyes at the Clam Box, already shivering yet still polite.

Likable boy.

It was a dry cold, a snowless night, and Nick, so exposed in the Crosley, hurt driving into it. The starless sky was friendly, and the moon, if there was one, was wide.

Kathryn Scanlan

Two Fictions

FLORIDA IS FOR LOVERS

My parents wanted me out from the start. In good weather they turned me out at dawn to wander from door to door. The neighbor women whose children were grown took a special liking to me. They held me on their laps and fed me sticky rolls and milky coffee while they smoked and told me about their husbands. Then, at dusk – with resignation – my parents would unlock their door and shoo me inside.

What they did all day every day, I didn't know. I watched them come and go from the shrubs across the street. Some days my mother left in the car or on foot, carrying sacks when she returned. She often sat unmoved for hours at the kitchen table, but then she would suddenly rise and dart quickly from room to room.

When my father left he usually did not return until very late at night or a day or two later. Sometimes he came back fresh as he'd gone – a shaven nut-colored man in a smooth wool sport coat – but on occasion he returned haggard and mean with a cut above his eye or a swollen cheek or hand, his coat lost, his undershirt reeking.

They kept me in the basement in a large room with a tiled floor and windows that looked onto the ground of the back yard, where I watched their sandaled feet cross and uncross in the grass.

When they rid themselves of me at last – when we three stood on the cement slab out front looking at one another — my father said, Wait. He went into the garage and came out holding a wire cage with two small green birds in it. They were on sale, he said.

I put the cage on the passenger seat of my car and buckled it in. As I drove, the birds made a continual racket — not song, not a recognizable call of any kind — something hostile and harsh, like the wild shriek of a security alarm. I was unable to tell whether it was directed toward me, toward one another, or toward the sky that passed above them out the window and the other birds they saw — if they saw them — strung on cables and perched on light posts, or else drifting in slow, aimless circles.

Then, I carried them up the steps to the apartment I'd rented and set the cage on the floor.

I consulted a book and determined the smaller, less attractive bird to be the male. He tormented the female relentlessly — unless she liked that kind of thing. He bit her neck and hustled her into a corner, where they scuffled and exchanged bitter sounds. When I refreshed their little dishes of seeds and water, he always ate first — making a mess she would clean up.

He wouldn't let me touch him, but if I put a steady hand into the cage, she would come into it and sit placidly a while.

I sometimes set them loose in the bathroom. They flew straight to the window and fell stunned from the glass to the smooth slope of tub below. Their cries echoed on the tile, sounding like a dozen desperate birds. They gnawed the top of my shower curtain ragged and dripped their marbled waste everywhere.

I found that if I threw a large, heavy cloth over their cage, they became quiet in the sudden darkness and did not stir again until I lifted it. I would sometimes leave them in the dark for days to allow my head to clear. Then I would fling them into cruel daylight. Stunned, sedated, squinting – that was when I loved them most, if I ever loved them. I would take the female in my hand, my fingers curling around her body, which looked soft and plump but felt hollow and bristled. Her heart would shudder wildly beneath my thumb.

At some point, she stopped eating. She sat on the dirty floor of the cage all day, and when he harassed her she did not fight back. He knocked her onto her side again and again. Eventually, she did not get up. Then he left her alone.

After dark I dug a shallow hole beneath the arbor vitae near the front steps of my building. I placed her body – wrapped in toilet paper – into it.

When I left for work the next morning, the brown grass was bright with shreds of tropical green. I crouched to where her rigid body lay headless and half-chewed. From the window of the first-floor apartment, a fat white cat opened its mouth – a small black cavern on a snowy hillside.

I stood looking at him in his cage. He climbed up and down the bars like a maniac. When I came closer, he came closer. When I extended the tip of my index finger, he closed his beak greedily around it, which hurt, but not as much as I'd expected.

A few years later, my parents died – one after the other – from swift, unforeseen causes. My three elder siblings – the eldest more than twenty years my senior – drove from the places they lived and loaded their cars with the things they wanted. They'd spent years compiling detailed lists and went home happy.

My sister gave me a key to the house when she left. The key was threaded onto a fob in the shape of a smiling pink dolphin. 'FLORIDA IS FOR LOVERS' was stamped on its body in a rainbow font.

I let myself in by the formal front door they never used. I hung my jacket and bag onto an empty coat rack. I wiped my shoes on the rug.

There was a very still, sun-cooked smell in the house. I went to the long, marble-topped, mirror-backed cabinet where they kept their bottles and glasses. I offered myself a drink, which I accepted.

With my cut crystal tumbler of brandy, I sat in my mother's upholstered reading chair. *A History of English Country Houses* lay on the stand, bisected by a thick, tasseled bookmark. Her potted plants, I saw, would not last.

I offered myself another drink, this time with a cube of ice and a sweet biscuit from a tin in the cupboard. I went upstairs. I sat on the edge of my mother's bed, which was neatly made.

On her dresser was her jewelry box – a lacquered stack of drawers that opened and closed on hidden hinges. My sister took her diamond shoulder dusters, her Italian choker. But here was a gold chain hooked to a round locket with a tiny photograph of a man – not my father – inside. Here was a thick silver ring set with a large black stone that streaked orange when I slipped it onto my finger.

In my father's room, in the ashtray on his nightstand, was a half-smoked cigarette. His sportcoat hung sloppily from his desk chair. I sat in the chair and reached into his pockets. Inside were wads of ones and fives. I opened his desk drawers, beginning at the top. In the bottommost one lay a tiny pistol with a mother of pearl handle. It looked like a toy, and might have been.

I went back downstairs and got my jacket and bag. I locked the house and drove to the apartment I now shared with a man I'd met waiting for a bus. On the turnpike, I rolled my window down and tossed the tumbler. It split on the pavement, then disappeared beneath the wheels of a big rig.

When I arrived, the apartment was dark and quiet. I took the ring from my finger and lifted the locket over my head. I unkinked the bills. I removed the pistol from my pocket. I spaced everything evenly across the dining table. He came up behind me and put his hands on my neck.

I've just robbed a place, I said.

Looks like there wasn't much to take, he said, squeezing me in a way I'd come – after many years of failed attempt – to enjoy.

SMALL PINK FEMALE

I've courted in the traditional fashion, of course – coming together on evenings arranged in advance, in the dark, on padded seats, facing the huge brash rectangle, or else in simulated candlelight, knees tucked beneath a drooping white cloth, enduring protracted sessions of mastication and, later, abbreviated fornication.

Then, on a fine afternoon – sprung loose from any duty or thought – I found myself in the far corner of a florist's shop, sniffing around. From behind an enormous pittosporum emerged a small pink female, neatly aproned. I let her lead me to her chilled case of product. Here were entities that had unfurled slowly, elongated steadily – until severed.

The odor of that place – it did something to me. I love you, I said, and handed her all of my money. I walked stiffly out the door, clutching the cold bundle to my chest, shoving my face into the top. From the bottom, it leaked gently onto my arm.

Later, in private, I undid the wrapping and gazed at the gangly splay across my table. Some positioning was necessary – as well as some trimming, pinching, plucking and shoving – to reveal their best advantage.

I did glimpse her once more – little, bulbous, waddling slightly ahead of me, her hair like a toasted dinner roll on the back of her head – and I ran forward gasping. I flung a wild arm and spun her by the shoulder and dropped to my knees. I grabbed a plump hand. Please! I shouted. I'd never been happier.

But I've made bad choices from the start – ask any of my associates. In my temperate apartment, the heads relaxed one by one – then burst in fits of yellow dander. And oh, how quickly they shriveled then – falling limply as wads of used tissue, issuing no scent whatever.

REMEMBERING

HOB BROUN

1950 - 1987

Heywood Orren (or 'Hob') Broun published three books in his brief lifetime – *Odditorium* (1983), *Inner Tube* (1985) and *Cardinal Numbers* (1988) – none of which are well known today. But Broun's intense, eccentric fictions ought to be more than a mere footnote to literary history. In this, the first of a semi-regular series on neglected writers, *Egress* celebrates Broun's life and work. Kevin McMahon reflects on his close friendship with the author, while Sam Lipsyte describes his formative encounter with Broun's fiction. *Egress* is also pleased to present a selection of pages from Broun's personal journal – a vivid and often hilarious record of a brilliant mind at play.

IMPRESSIONS OF HOB
Kevin McMahon

I first met Hob in September 1968. We were both entering freshmen newly arrived at Reed College in Portland, Oregon. Checking out the campus on the first day, I found my way to the Commons, the student union, which contained a game room with professional quality pool tables. The usual dubious characters were hanging around, including Hob, who on this occasion was wearing a well-creased leather jacket, a mesh t-shirt of the kind favored by street hustlers, blue jeans faded and ripped at the knee, and alligator wing tips. Around his neck was a miniature ivory skull on a leather thong. He was a hawk-nosed, skinny little guy with lank, scraggly long hair, spidery and angular, his movements precise as he worked the table sinking one ball after another. His hands were noticeably fine – a musician's hands, with long tapering fingers, on which he wore a couple of rather gaudy Mafioso-quality rings. I remember thinking he couldn't possibly be a student – he looked like an aging juvenile delinquent working hard at becoming a career criminal. I accepted the challenge of a game. Hob of course wanted to make it interesting, but being short of cash it was proposed that we play for record albums, and in this way got to talking music, likes, dislikes, hatreds and objects of contempt, the kind of antler rubbing by which young guys got acquainted in those days. I gathered that my first impression of Hob was wrong.

He was a student here, too, also from back east – a native Manhattanite. I'd attended boarding school in New England, Hob the Dalton School in New York, and it turned out we knew some of the same people through these connections. It quickly became evident that, to an unusual degree even for the type of highly opinionated, one-upping prep school boys I was used to, Hob was not only emphatic about music, he was indifferent to *nothing*.

After hustling me out of a slew of albums, Hob invited me over to his dorm. Somehow, he'd brought two big steamer trunks packed solid with LPs with him from New York. They must have weighed a ton apiece. An older couple were already in the room, whom Hob introduced as 'Woodie and Jane'. These were his parents. I recognized Woodie right away as Heywood Hale Broun, who was pretty well-known for his eccentric TV sports featurettes, which he delivered on-air wearing a crazy quilt sport jacket, eyes crinkled in wintry amusement over a Bowery saloonkeeper's moustache. This is how I learned Hob's last name, without having to ask. (His full name was Heywood Orren Broun, but I never heard anyone call him Heywood. I believe Orren was his maternal grandfather's name.) Woodie was mixing gimlets in a cocktail shaker and serving them up in martini glasses. Hob's mother Jane, a petite, well-preserved blonde, was perched on the desk with her legs neatly crossed. A former actress, she retained an air of the theatrical that on her was charming rather than affected. They were all very easy with each other, and it seemed to me that the Brouns were more like intimate friends than parents and child, three against the world.

Hob was well aware that he came from cultural aristocracy, and proud of it, but he didn't wear it on his sleeve. His grandfather was Heywood Broun, the newspaper columnist who was one of the founders of the Algonquin Round Table, and his grandmother was Ruth Hale, famous in her day as a pioneering militant feminist, and also a charter member of the Algonquin. They were resolutely unconventional parents, and I think Woodie strove mightily to avoid repeating their mistakes, while keeping the basic bohemian ideal. In consequence, Hob didn't have much to rebel against at home, and he seemed miraculously well-adjusted to me.

Judging from photographs, I'd say that physically Hob took more after his grandmother's side of the family. His eyes, especially, were very much like Ruth's, and his hawk nose appears to be a distinctive Hale characteristic, although he had the Broun forehead. His lineage was mostly Scottish with some German, and of course Welsh on his mother's side. Through her, Frank Lloyd Wright was a distant relation and Hob did resemble his famous cousin in size, artistic perfectionism and pugnacity. I once visited Wright's Hollyhock House in East Hollywood with Hob, and he found it amusing that I had to stoop while he strolled right through the architect's Wright-sized doorways and halls. We were Mutt and

Jeff, he liked to say, after the tall and short hobo pals in the old comic strip.

Hob and I were fast friends, and later on became roommates when we rented an off-campus apartment together in a crumbling stucco triplex next to the freight yards –uncoupled boxcars slamming into each other went on more or less every night. Our landlady was a querulous widow named Maude Butts, whose apartment was right across the hall, and who came to hate us in short order. Our only other neighbor was an older Ghanaian exchange student with a wife and child, whose answer to every problem was 'I will get my two-two and shoot them!' These types of characters were Hob's primary object of study. From childhood, he never intended to be anything but a writer. His powers of observation were keen, and he was very penetrating about small differences. He didn't tolerate pretentiousness and phoniness at all, and wasn't shy about letting people know it. I was on the receiving end of his lash a couple of times myself.

In college, Hob wasn't much interested in radical politics, and enjoyed mocking the New Left types on campus, such as one purportedly working class kid from Detroit who styled himself a 'White Panther' and had a small troop of impressionable coeds he would march around the quad in quasi-military formation. Hob named them the 'Buttock Power' brigade. He also had a kind of genial contempt for campus hippies whom he considered mostly fakes and saw mainly as useful for scoring weed. In general he avoided hard drugs. He preferred to keep his mind sharp. It was his instrument and he took care of it. If he identified with any kind of sociopolitical grouping at all it would have been the Beats, as an indigenous American literary movement. Reed was visited by a few counterculture heroes in our time there. Hob wasn't excited about any of them. He wasn't the type to be star-struck and preferred to form his own judgments.

In New York the Brouns owned an apartment on West 81st Street just off Central Park, which is where Hob grew up. It was cozy and old-fashioned, not over-large, of course un-air conditioned in summer and heated by ironwork radiators in winter, a typical pre-war Manhattan flat. They had a pair of lovable old dogs, mixed-breed collies named Daisy and Buttercup. The park in back of the Hayden Planetarium was across the street, and Hob would walk the dogs there so they could relieve themselves. Hob was a pretty heavy drinker in his teens and twenties, and we went on some epic pub crawls together in the city, but he gave it up around the time he turned thirty. I think he was worried it was interfering with his writing, or maybe he just got tired of it. At any rate, not long afterwards he told me that the mere smell of alcohol now made him sick.

Hob dropped out of Reed at the end of sophomore year. He drew a high number in the draft lottery, and figured he'd wasted enough time in college. He didn't need a bachelor's degree to write. In the following years, we always kept in touch and on occasion he'd drop in while passing through. He seemed to be in more or less constant motion around the country, soaking up 'the old, weird America' that no longer exists. He drove a boxy piece of pre-owned seventies Detroit iron with a manual shift and no handbrake, and a roomy dashboard with a grid of small square spaces into which Hob inserted tiny model railroad type plastic figures of people, farm animals, a water tower, palm trees and the like, so he had a miniature landscape to gaze over while driving down the road. He liked small things, little pocket worlds like that. He was sensitive about his height, but he also enjoyed deprecating it himself rather than letting others get the jump on him. Sometimes he even shopped for clothes in the children's section. In San Francisco I rented a room for a time in a Victorian shotgun flat. When Hob came to stay for a bit he moved into the hall closet, pushing the hanging coats aside to fit in a cot for himself, and setting his typewriter on a funky end table. This was the treasured old-school manual he carried everywhere in his travels. Hob never learned to touch-type, he jack-hammered the keys with his two index fingers, a menthol cigarette, Newport or Kool, clenched between his teeth. And there he remained for a couple of weeks, working on his novel with that singleness of purpose that I always envied. His face took on an expression of focused, almost angry intensity when engaged in serious pursuits - writing or gambling, shooting pool, ice skating, chopping garlic and onions. He was highly competitive and hated to lose. This went for his writing, too. He measured himself against other authors past and present. He was perversely proud of his stack of rejection slips from *The New Yorker*, but it rankled him at the same time. He felt he rightly belonged in that company, but like Groucho simultaneously considered it beneath him to apply to a club that would take him as a member.

I can't bear to write too much about the end of Hob's story. In his early thirties he was a published author with a promising future ahead, in full control of his instrument, and he'd finally found the love of his life, and this time she loved him back. Then he was stricken with paralysis, the result of an operation to remove a tumor wrapped around his spinal column. He woke up from it in a wheelchair, unable to move anything below the top of his shoulders, his every breath provided by a tracheostomy tube connected to a ventilator. I know that in those first days and weeks he would have preferred to die on the table, but over time sheer grit and strength of character saw him through. I also think his pride was a factor – he refused to be an object of pity to anyone. Thanks to a then-primitive computer keyboard operable by a breath-controlled device, he was able to keep writing, and did. I don't think he would have made it otherwise, through the additional time he was granted before death took him suddenly in the middle of the night by acute cardio-respiratory failure, caused by the regrowth of that tumor. It was close to Christmas, 1987. He was thirty-seven years old.

The Brouns kept a country house just outside of Woodstock upstate, a comfortable, rambling, lived-in cottage stuffed with books and souvenirs from Woodie's travels and career, where they felt most at home and spent the summers and winter holidays. The picture window in the dining room looked out on a great swath of meadow and the Catskills beyond. Across the road they had another tract of woods, surrounding a large pond with a little island in the center, good for swimming in summer and ice skating in the winter months. Hob was an avid skater, a regular Hans Brinker, and would spend hours at it, hands behind his back and bent at the waist, cutting arcs across the knobbly surface of his frozen pond, round and round as the sun went down. That's the image of him I'm keeping.

$R_1 = H$ or SO_2ONa
$R_2 = SO_2ONa$ or H

The Rockefeller University 1901
PRO·BONO·HUMANI·GENERIS

1230 YORK AVENUE · NEW YORK, N.Y. 10021

ALIENATION & ANXIETY

PLEASE BREAK UP
INTO GROUPS AND
DISCUSS

The projections of human experience in thought or social institutions are misleadingly separated from man in abstract speculation and acquire a harmful power over him, divide him from himself & others so that he is never truly whole, never truly 'at home.'

IF BRAIN ACTION IS TO BE EXPLAINED IN TERMS OF THE FORMATION AND FIRING OF SPECIFIC, YET DYNAMIC, NEURONAL CIRCUITS, HOW ARE THE APPROPRIATE CIRCUIT CONNECTIONS MADE?????????????????????

1) List dependence oriented kinds of anxiety and give examples from your own life.

2) Contrast Hegel's Philosophy of State with Doleman's Imperative of Ficticious Politics.

For solutions and suggested reading
PLEASE FOLD OUT

$S = \frac{1}{n-2}$

$N \cdot (x_{61} - y_i) \sqrt{} \geq 3.4$

Daydreaming?

Zero-Base Media Planning.

$\hat{\xi} \rightarrow (x_{61} - \bar{x})^2$

75

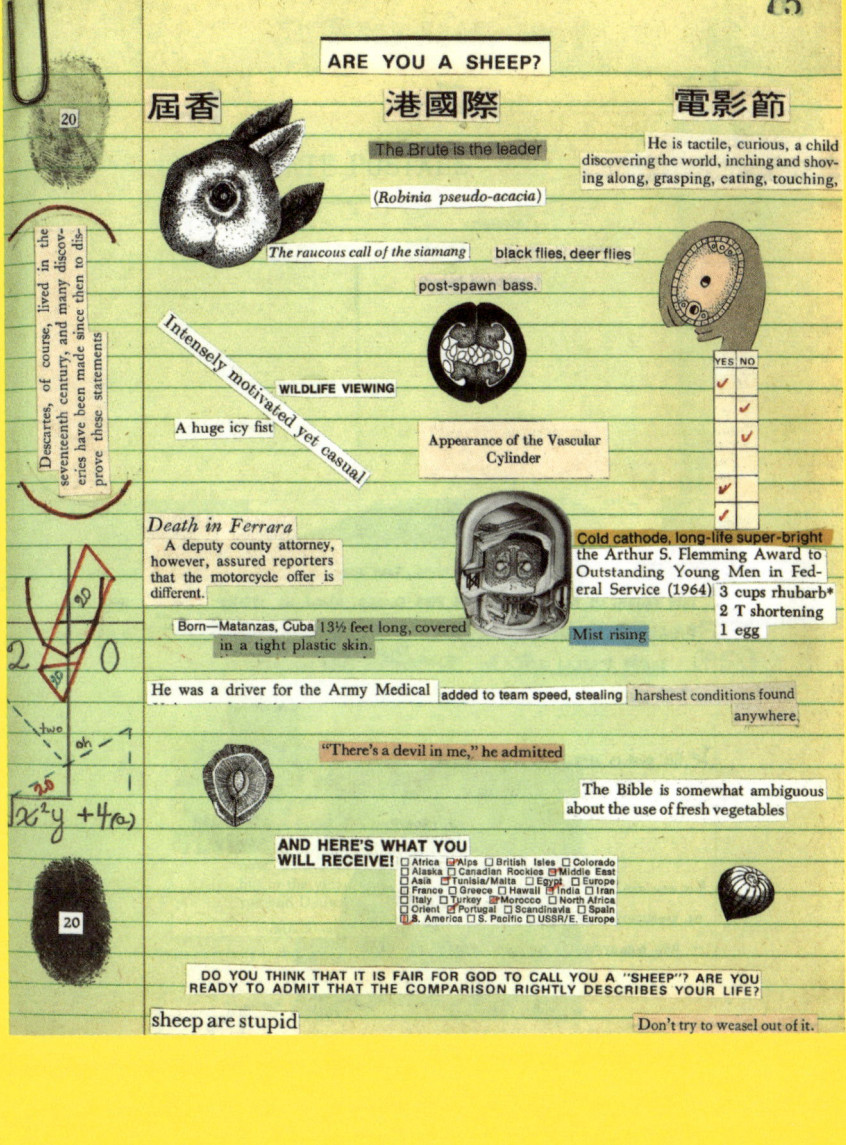

ARE YOU A SHEEP?

屆香　　港國際　　　　電影節

The Brute is the leader

He is tactile, curious, a child discovering the world, inching and shoving along, grasping, eating, touching,

(Robinia pseudo-acacia)

The raucous call of the siamang　　black flies, deer flies

post-spawn bass.

Descartes, of course, lived in the seventeenth century, and many discoveries have been made since then to disprove these statements

Intensely motivated yet casual

WILDLIFE VIEWING

A huge icy fist

Appearance of the Vascular Cylinder

	YES	NO
	✓	
		✓
		✓
		✓
	✓	

Death in Ferrara

A deputy county attorney, however, assured reporters that the motorcycle offer is different.

Cold cathode, long-life super-bright

the Arthur S. Flemming Award to Outstanding Young Men in Federal Service (1964)　3 cups rhubarb*
2 T shortening
1 egg

Born—Matanzas, Cuba　13½ feet long, covered in a tight plastic skin.

Mist rising

He was a driver for the Army Medical　added to team speed, stealing　harshest conditions found anywhere.

"There's a devil in me," he admitted

The Bible is somewhat ambiguous about the use of fresh vegetables

AND HERE'S WHAT YOU WILL RECEIVE!
☐ Africa ☒ Alps ☐ British Isles ☐ Colorado
☐ Alaska ☐ Canadian Rockies ☒ Middle East
☐ Asia ☒ Tunisia/Malta ☐ Egypt ☐ Europe
☐ France ☐ Greece ☐ Hawaii ☒ India ☐ Iran
☐ Italy ☐ Turkey ☒ Morocco ☐ North Africa
☐ Orient ☒ Portugal ☐ Scandinavia ☐ Spain
☒ S. America ☐ S. Pacific ☐ USSR/E. Europe

DO YOU THINK THAT IT IS FAIR FOR GOD TO CALL YOU A "SHEEP"? ARE YOU READY TO ADMIT THAT THE COMPARISON RIGHTLY DESCRIBES YOUR LIFE?

sheep are stupid　　　　　　　　　　　　　Don't try to weasel out of it.

WISE CRACK BAR SIGNS

Some is for eating now

---GLOBUS FALLS   The Society for the Advancement of Nordic Casuistry will hold its biannual conclave this Tuesday evening at 7 PM in the main banquet hall of Gulbenkian's Red Vest Inn, Cortez Avenue, Globus Corners. The Guest Speaker at the Tuesday meeting will be Col. Theron (Bud) Parmesan, Ret., the noted Swedenborgian, who will explore the topic, "Under The Wheels Of History." Col. Parmesan served one and on half terms as Superintendent of Highways for Globus County in the late '60's. Following his talk, Col. Parmesan will make the presentation of the Gustaf II Medal for Outstanding Nordic Fortitude to a local student whose name was unavailable at press time. We do have tentative menu information at this time. Due to complaints from the last gettogether, the soup course will be eliminated. The main entree will be Lutheran Game Pie a la Fifi with Piped Potatoes and Carrot Coins. A film will be shown at 9 PM, "The Eye And Mind Of Husserl: Beyond Perception." There will be ample parking, possibly. Tickets are $5.00 in advance, $6.50 at the door.

the trigger for murder

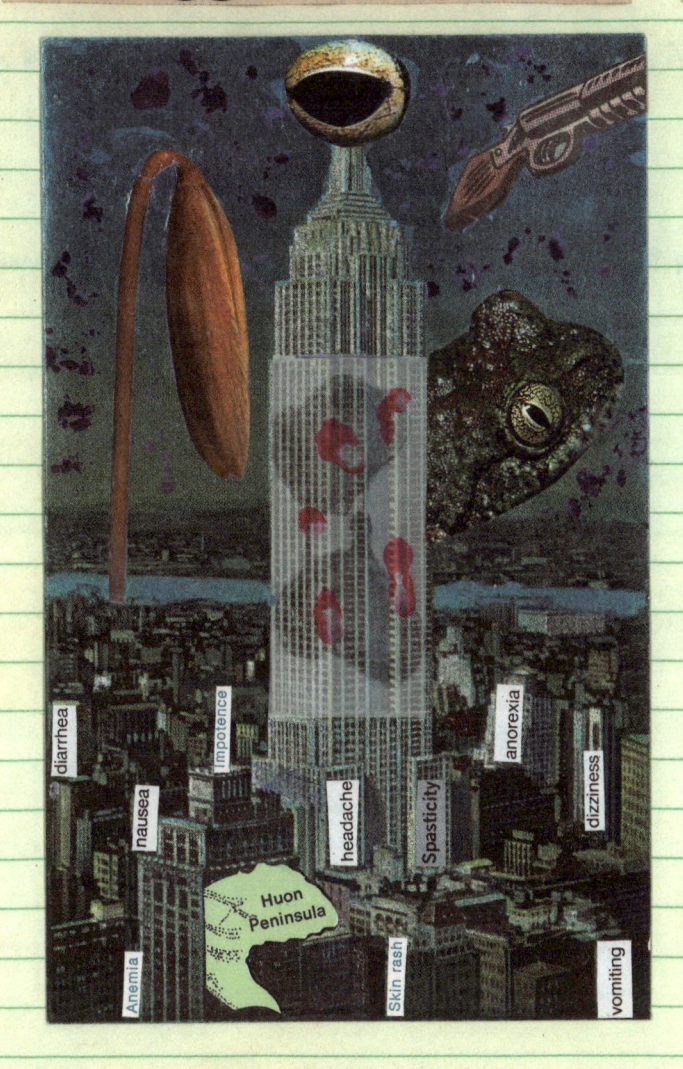

- diarrhea
- nausea
- Anemia
- impotence
- headache
- Huon Peninsula
- Spasticity
- Skin rash
- anorexia
- dizziness
- vomiting

URBAN ANOREXIASCAPE #1

Mrs. Falco is here to have her underarms waxed. A late appointment, lights out in the front hall, drapes pulled. Radio noise from out of the shadows: Martin Block's Make Believe Ballroom. Mrs. Falco reaches into her red plush handbag, brings out a circular mirror with tobacco shreds magnetized to the glass. She holds it up close, fogging it with her breath. Her lips are chapped, peeling. Mrs. Falco lights an Old Gold, blows smoke in a thin stream from the corner of her mouth. She is prickly hot and woozy (that pastrami on the way over? gunk under the waiter's nails) and slides out of her Persian lamb. *** "Hiya, Mrs. F. Take off your shoes, why don't you. We'll both relax." Norma comes out of the back room -- dim reflections in the glass fronted cabinets, a cold chemical aroma -- crosses the pink carpet in her blunt nurse's shoes. White shoes, white hose, white smock. She adjusts a pile of towels, aligns the bottles and implements on a shelf. Then turns slowly around, all blank. Mrs. Falco experiences an unpleasant tingle, a fear reflex in the blood. With a ruptured logic that attracts her, she envisions Norma coming for her with a shiny instrument. So many of them here: needles and blades, shanks of metal, miniature rakes, scrapers, scoops, probes, things with curving plastic spikes at the end. Coming for her with slit eyes and narrow, clammy hands that smell of bleach. *** "I think I need to lie down." Mrs. Falco's fluttering hands go to her face. *** "That's okay, honey, just you leave it to me." Norma guides her to one of the large blue chairs, presses a foot pedal to activate its pneumatic lifts and tilts. *** Mrs. Falco smiles weakly. "Be gentle, darling." *** "Ain't I always." Norma clasps the chloroform impregnated scarf over Mrs. Falco's face. After a moment, her hands dusted with rice flour, working from the bottom up, she unbuttons Mrs. Falco's blouse.

868 ESTELLE TAYLOR AND JACK DEMPSEY AT THEIR BEAUTIFUL HOME IN LAUGHLIN PARK, HOLLYWOOD

Dempsey knelt and dabbled his fingers in the velvety waters of the pool. The silvery light of a three quarter moon broke through the palms. Valdez, the butler, was just now beginning to take down the Japanese lanterns, to sweep the ashes and cigarette butts, the trampled canapes and swizzle sticks, from the flagstones.

Dempsey slid out of his tux and rolled up the sleeves of his starched white shirt. As he plunged his arm into the water, he thought of rainbow trout spawning high in the Poncha Mountains overlooking Manassas, Colorado; the icy, glistening headwaters of the Lizard Tail river and a fresh breeze in the aspens.

A nasal, insistent voice from the portico: "Jackie, you better come inside. Jack? Come on, let's go to bed."

It was Estelle. So recently the ritzy hostess with the fried hair and the fancy footwork...That ten piece band was going to cost. And the swan carved from ice and packed with caviar.

"What's the matter with you, Jack? Are you drunk?"

Dempsey turned and stared over the clipped lawn, through the damp, faintly stirring shadows at its edge, and beyond. He thought of a wild, black-eyed Hopi girl and their meeting place at the flat rock under the pines.

101

RHUMBA!   ANSWER THE CALL OF THE DANCE-SONG CRAZE   **JITTERBUG!**

Flip back the folds. See the loose, extinct geysers of alkaline soda.

KEEP THOSE TOUGH HOMBRES IN THE SHOP IN LINE!

You must, however, assist Nature to an electronically controlled swig of water

Alan Alda confessed to murder of pretty bobby-soxer collapsed during his own crucifixion after the hike through the white-hot embers.

Growth, not decay, led to corruption in pure silk or lustrous rayon.

Start with 1 pound of oxtails

Obtain the Property Report required by Federal law

Crane says you're a stickler for quality. The quality of hand-wrapped rattan.

So indulge yourself.

Setting aside for the moment **BIG GAME** and **SMALL GAME**

PENDING YOUR RECEIPT OF spray from the sponge

Don't breathe a word about Rumored inference that naked ear is immodest

Don't refer to a dynamic way of life

YOU ARE WONDERFUL IN DEATH

!! MALDITA POBREZA !!
!! MALDITA IGNORANCIA !!

HOB BROUN
Sam Lipsyte

Hob Broun's been dead a long time. I've been reading him for longer. When I was about sixteen, I found his novel *Inner Tube* on my father's desk. Broun's father and mine were friendly and the younger Broun had written to my father, a journalist and novelist, for advice. I took the book off to another room and in a couple of hours I had a new hero. Another thrill arrived when my father shared the part of one letter where Broun mentioned me, hoped I would survive coming of age in the 'cynical and feckless eighties'. That formulation still ricochets around my mind, mostly when I hear the word 'feckless', or somebody mentions the 1980s. It happens more often than I ever expected.

Broun didn't leave that much behind, but he left enough, his sentences so rich, so chuggy-jam (a phrase I later learned with delight from Broun's editor, and my teacher, Gordon Lish) with sound, image, thought, feeling. If a poet bequeathed to the world the same amount of pages we'd consider it a fairly sizable body of work. Hob Broun was pretty much of a poet: 'I am a man in early middle age, precise to a fault in my habits, but given no less to loose talk. My marriage is nine years old. I am lugubrious; Daphne is the one with fizz.' By poet, I don't mean one who writes in a particular scheme differentiated from prose, but rather a writer looking to manage every word for maximum sonic and emotional effect. All writers, on their best days, aspire to the condition of poetry. That's not quite how Walter Pater had it, I know. But Pater didn't write his best work while sipping and puffing through a plastic tube, one letter at a time. Broun, a quadriplegic for the last seven years of his brief life, did.

(All able-bodied writers who whine about the 'slog of revision' should just go ahead and die.)

Hob Broun was also pretty much of a novelist. He sure as hell knew how to open one: 'You're not going to like this, but some years ago, in the family room of the house where I grew up in Lake Success, New York my mother cancelled an unrelenting life by plunging her head through the twenty-six-inch screen of a Motorola color television.' No, we're certainly not going to like this. But some of us will forever love it, and not just for the startle, the bold attack, the layering of shock, grotesquerie, pathos, wit in a single paragraph. Yes, Lake Success, how wonderfully apt, and 'cancel', of course, that's what they do to failed TV programs, but it's Broun's ear that also impresses, the way the acoustic moments necessitate each other, the relations among 'you're' and 'like this' and 'Lake Success, New York', how 'Motorola' spawns both 'color' and 'television'.

Speaking of television, that beginning is from *Inner Tube*, and Broun always wrote with unrivalled edge and humor about the indoctrination modern American consciousness received through screens, big and small. The vast wasteland, for Broun's narrator, is lover and progenitor. (He earns the method of that mother's suicide over and over again.) Some of Broun prefigures more recent fiction, with intimate, detail-steeped scenes bleeding into more essayistic modes heavy on cultural critique, and some of Broun isn't like that at all, but his prose always comes with a stance, at a slant, with a vulnerable, visceral charge. His narratives are also often laced with Broun's deep feel for older versions of modernity. Video players and player pianos were both objects he might lavish language upon, and if you desire instruction on how to acknowledge in your fiction the funny and forlorn ways popular culture seeps into our inmost zones without becoming slavish to its properties, study Broun's approach.

At his published zenith, in the story collection *Cardinal Numbers,* Broun ranged across genres and voices at a dizzying rate – savoring more than one flavor of pulp – but every story, no matter its historical provenance or structural gambit, is easily traceable, because the sentences are so wildly precise, the observations so mordant and empathetic at once. To stray a little from one over-quoted dictum, Broun makes the strange stranger, yet also ferries the familiar back from the bogs of contempt to felt, human realms.

So much of it still sticks. Even today, if somebody says his name, the first thing I picture is not the author himself but his character Schenk, the old, antiquarian book dealer, drinking a glass of ice water on a cold, winter day, letting the cubes fall against his teeth. Then maybe I'll flash on the bunkhouse *ménage à trois* among gritty gunslingers in Broun's Old West trope-shredder 'Blood Aspens', and after that recall the delicate devastation at the close of 'Rosella, in Stages', the impossible way Broun summons, syntactically, the last crackles of memory and longing in a woman during her demented dying. Maybe I'll land on the scene where the narrator eats his pet goat in the desert at the finish of *Inner Tube* ('Rosing was good, fibrous but succulent'), puts his belongings to flame. He's now at the end of the given world: 'It is necessary to set myself out of motion, to disremember the automatic commands I have followed for so long, so many years of willfulness and waste. No more deconstruction or synopsis. Only pure unbroken signal. I open wide and it comes in so loud and clear that I twinge all up and down.'

Everything begins and ends with such twinges, brought on by Broun's signals, his utterance, blown one particle at a time. That there is more to read is a welcome miracle. I mean to go on reading Hob Broun, in all my stages.

Diane Williams

The Important Transport

Otto told me that our opportunity had been squandered and that I should have felt compelled to contribute something. He said, 'It is too bad you don't understand what is happening here.'

And, I saw that it was true – that I had failed to do my best.

This was to be our short interregnum. How to proceed next?

That morning the wake-up radio music alarm had been set, but the volume knob had been wrenched by somebody, counter-clockwise, full-on. My first thought was that the window must be open and that the wind had caught at the blinds and that it was blowing across the fins – the slats, rather – and that they were vibrating and causing this tremendous sound before it dawned on me that this blast was something other and it made me afraid.

And, where did Otto go? He was missing and the window was indeed open and a small breeze lightly batted the venetian blind's liftcord tassel against the wall.

In an hour he was back again and the look on his face was one of gratitude, and to add to this comforting effect, he smiled.

'Where did you go?' I asked.

'Kay,' he said. That's my name.

'You're all I have. Where did you go?'

'Do you like it here?' he said.

'No, I don't like it here. Why should I?'

'I know. I know,' he said. 'Some water?' He had to walk and to walk, to go such a short way, it seemed, to get that for me.

We had another such dialogue the next day.

'Do I have to say?' he said.

'Yes,'

'Suzette.'

'Oh, Suzette,' I said.

Later on he married the young girl.

I have had to wait for my own happiness. I married Eric Throssel, who is a good companion – and I thought I was very happy when we had finished supper one night. But the more important transport occurred en route to Long Grove while I was driving.

Eric spoke, and his words I don't remember them, but thank God they served to release the cramping in my neck, and in my shoulders and my back and they provided for an unexpected increased intake of oxygen. Can we leave it at that?

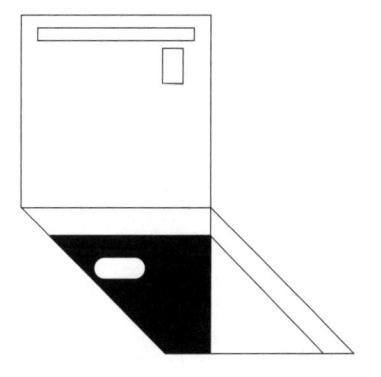

Evan Lavender-Smith

Two Unknowns

_____ creates an infinitely hot and dense singularity – which expands – quite fast – then begins to slow – and continues to slow – everything begins to cool – to slow and to cool – until such time as inflation begins – and the universe expands – quite fast – it expands exponentially – until such time as inflation ends – and the universe cools – and continues to cool – it cools to a quark-gluon plasma – some of the quarks begin to combine with some of the gluons – forming baryons – more of the quarks combine with more of the gluons – forming more baryons – baryons such as protons and neutrons – some of these protons combine with some of these neutrons – forming deuterium – and helium nuclei – and more of these protons combine with more of these neutrons – forming more deuterium – and more helium nuclei – now some electrons combine with some helium nuclei – forming atoms – and more electrons combine with more helium nuclei – forming even more atoms – atoms combine with atoms – forming matter – more atoms combine with more atoms – forming more matter – now there are more atoms combining – now there's more matter forming – as well as gas clouds – gas clouds, which start collapsing – now even more gas clouds are collapsing – and now they start condensing, the gas clouds do – more and more gas clouds condense – the remaining gas and dust begin to collect together – they continue collecting together, the remaining gas and dust do – and they continue to do this – until such time as some of this dust–gas mixture begins clumping into little asteroids – and into even more little asteroids – then a bunch of these little asteroids begin clumping into a bunch of little planets – and now into a bunch more little planets – even more little planets – some of which little planets start clumping into fewer, larger planets – and into fewer, larger planets – and into even fewer, even larger planets – into fewer – into larger – fewer – larger – etc. – and then – on one of these planets – after a certain one of these planets has been spinning around for some time – for quite some time – something happens – something rather interesting – this planet's atmosphere – it was an extremely turbulent atmosphere, at the time – an atmosphere composed primarily of hydrogen, oxygen, carbon dioxide, hydrogen sulfide, and nitrogen – maybe a little carbon monoxide – maybe throw a little methane into the mix, if you want – this atmosphere – exposed, as it was, to various forms of energy – such as lightning – such as sunlight – begins producing simple organic compounds – just monomers, nothing much – monomers which begin concentrating at various locations around this interesting little planet – at this little planet's especially scenic locations – oceanic vents, shorelines, etc. – and then the little monomers begin combining with other little monomers – little monomers combine with other little monomers – now more little monomers are combining with even more little monomers – creating more complex organic compounds – little polymers, nothing much – just some little polymers – but then something happens to these polymers – something rather interesting – the little polymers transform into cells – magically, it would seem – into protocells, if you will – cells containing RNA – but how did this happen? – well, it wasn't magic, to tell you the truth – it was all fairly straightforward – nucleotides were necessary, that's all – you add a little water into the mix – maybe a little energy source – a skosh of cyanide derivatives – a skosh of formaldehyde derivatives – no big deal – toss in a pinch of phosphate – all pretty volatile stuff – maybe some pond water evaporates, if you're lucky – and voila – sugar is now clinging to a nucleobase – you've got yourself a nucleotide – just like that – now the nucleotides begin to polymerize – no big deal – nothing much – and now you've got yourself a chain of them – and now you're going to want to fold the chain up – carefully – very carefully – fold that chain of nucleotides up just right – and it'll start catalyzing chemical reactions, if you're lucky – it just replicated itself – did you see? – and there it goes again – and again – look – what do you see? – it's totally different, all of a sudden – that's because it mutated – it's mutating every time it replicates, you may not have noticed – and once it starts mutating, there's really no stopping it – a little something called evolution kicks in – you're free to take a break – go to the bathroom – have yourself a drink – a cigarette – another drink – another cigarette – drinks combine with drinks – cigarettes with cigarettes – because once evolution gets hold of a catalyzing nucleotide, you're pretty much good to go – you can just kick back – and now you've got yourself an organism that's creating proteins – a little DNA, nothing much – and – as everybody knows – once you've got both RNA and DNA on your hands, you're pretty much good to go – now we can jump straight to prokaryotes – just some little prokaryotes – which evolve glycolysis – the ability to store energy in the chemical bonds of ATP – and the split between bacteria and archaea occurs – no big deal – nothing much – but then a certain bacterium decides to give a little something called photosynthesis a go – maybe try and generate a little ATP by exploiting a certain proton gradient – now we've got a photosynthesizing cyanobacteria on our hands – and look, over there – a few gazillion more of them – just carrying on – and then one day – wait for it – one day all the cyanobacteria on the planet get together and decide to throw a huge party – a party of truly staggering proportions – of epic, Burning Man proportions – a party that will later be referred to as the Great Oxidation Event – the cyanobacteria release gazillions of tons of oxygen in the atmosphere – eukaryotic cells appear – with their crazy orgies – orgies every day – orgies every minute – we're talking about literally gazillions of seedy eukaryotic sex orgies every minute of every day – now algae appears – dinoflagellates – protozoa – and then – wait for it – a little something called the ozone layer forms – now we've got fungi – we've got jellies –

we've got sponges – we've got corals – we've even got ourselves a few anemones – and then – hold on to your hat – chordates, arthropods, echinoderms, mollusks, brachiopods, foraminifers, radiolarians, graptolites, cephalopods, chitons, and – wait for it – we've got vertebrates – yes, you heard me correctly – vertebrates – and conodonts – and echinoids – we've got, no joke, plants moving onto land – fungi, too – now we've got spiders, we've got scorpions – we've even got fish growing teeth – why don't you mosey on over here and say hello to some of our lichens? – whatup, stoneworts? – whatup, harvestman, mites and hexapods? – ammonoids, we've even got some of them, too – now the first tetrapods move onto land – bugs are everywhere – some of them are even flying – get them off me, get them off – and sharks – yes, sharks – please mind the sharks – plants all over the place, I can barely see a thing – now we've got forests – and crabs and ferns – and ragfishes and hagfishes – and reptiles and beetles and – the Great Dying – sad stuff, I know – but now a nice little rejuvenating Marine Revolution rears its head – we've got ichthyosaurs, we've got gomphodont cynodonts, we've got rhynchosaurs – dinosaurs, too, and, wait – wait for it – oh my goodness, what are those? – mammals! – not to mention flies, turtles, viruses, hermit crabs, starfish, sponge reefs – and stegosauri – and salamanders – and newts – and don't forget the rays – and, yikes, blood-sucking insects – bees and snakes and tics and ants and now Another Big Dying – sad, sure, I know – but now conifers, conifers, conifers – and ginkgos, ginkgos, ginkgos – mammals, mammals, mammals – and birds – oh, what beautiful birds – we've got parrots, loons, swifts, woodpeckers – and bats – and butterflies – and moths – we've got grass – and pigs – we've got cats – we've got deer – we've got giraffes and hyenas and bears and kangaroos and tree sloths and hippopotami and mammoths and elephants and zebras and lions and – and – *Austrlopithecus* – and *Paranthropus* – and *Homo antecessor* – and *Homo heidelbergensis* – and *Homo neanderthalensis* – and – yes – *Homo sapiens* – and dogs – and *Homo sapiens* – and dogs – and *Homo sapiens* – and dogs – and *Homo sapiens* – and – did I mention dogs? – and *Homo sapiens* – *Homo sapiens* – *Homo sapiens* – *Homo sapiens* – and Coca-Cola products – the Coca-Cola Company is founded – and Pepsi products – Pepsi-Co is founded – and Hershey products – the Hershey Company is founded – and Apple products – Apple Computer, Inc., is incorporated – and then – wait – wait for it – a wee lad is born – just a wee lad – which wee lad grows – and grows – and grows – and fathers a wee lad of his own – and grows – and then a wee lass – and grows – and grows until such time as he writes the first draft of a book – and throws the draft in the trash can – and writes a second draft of the same book – and throws the second draft in the trash can – writes the third draft – trash can – fourth draft – trash can – fifth through the twenty-second drafts – trash can – but then later he reclaims the twenty-second draft from the trash – sends it to several publishers – he waits – rejected by all – throws the twenty-second draft in the trash can – writes the twenty-third draft – the twenty-fourth draft – the twenty-fifth draft – the twenty-sixth draft – all trashed – reclaims the twenty-sixth draft – sends it to several publishers – he waits – rejected – twenty-sixth draft – trash can – vows to quit writing forever – but then – after two whole days of not writing – he writes the twenty-seventh draft – the twenty-eight draft – the twenty-ninth draft – trash can – trash can – trash can – sends the reclaimed twenty-ninth to several publishers – rejection – rejection – rejection – the twenty-ninth draft is retrashed – again he vows to quit writing forever – three whole days – thirtieth draft – thirty-first draft – thirty-second draft – trash can – reclaimed, sent off – he waits – he waits – and – wait – wait for it – he opens his email inbox to find that he has received a tentative, conditional acceptance letter – yes! – his family throws him a shindig – pizza, couple-few 3-liter bottles of Mountain Dew – he rededicates himself – writes a brilliant thirty-third draft – blindly incorporating all editorial suggestions – emails the thirty-third draft to publisher – and wait – wait for it – draft approved! – another shindig – mac and cheese – 3-liter bottle of Mountain Dew – receives book contract via snailmail – signs book contract – mails it back – waits – book cover design arrives – shindig – mac and cheese – milk – he waits – publication date announced – he waits – publication date altered – waits – receives author proofs via snailmail – mac and cheese – proofreads author proofs – snailmails them back – waits – waits – oh, how he waits – and then – finally – publisher publishes book – two pizzas, four 3-liter bottles of Mountain Dew – and – wait – wait for it – a cake from Walmart with the title of his book spelled out in frosting script! – below the words Happy Birthday! – best family shindig ever – a family shindig of epic proportions – and then he waits a little longer – and – finally – at long last – the book is purchased – illegally downloaded – stolen – checked out – borrowed – thumbed through while browsing – and – wait – the book – wait for it – is read – is read delightfully – is read disdainfully – tearfully – laughingly – joyfully – sorrowfully – loathingly – by _____.

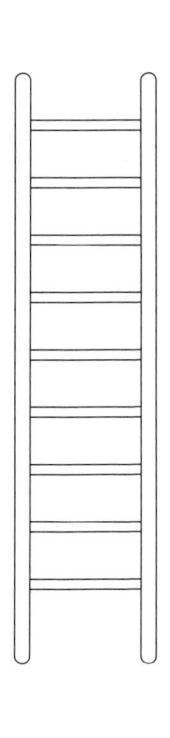

David Hayden

Two Fictions

CLIMBING

The sun was high and flat. Frost lay on the living world, a hard white was on the tarmac. Philip cycled down the path that ran beside the main road; screened by trees and bushes on one side, boundaried on the other by meadows that stretched across to the river and the woods. The spire of the cathedral rose out of the fields, the city both close and distant.

The tires slid, back and front, causing Philip to pull the bike under control so often that his wrists grew sore. When he arrived at the double-barred gate at the edge of the old wood he abandoned the road, lifted the bike over and passed through. The bike held steadier, the tires chewed through the scurf of frozen leaves that lay on the gravel trail. Philip sat back in the saddle and looked around at the empty wood. A row of redbrick block cottages flickered behind the trees until the path turned away from the village.

Philip dipped onto the handlebars and, to avoid a wide loop, steered off the trail and down a steep bank. He shifted gears to maintain momentum as he approached a tall, spreading yew at the bottom of the hollow. Silver and purple caught his eye from a cavity in the wide trunk. Philip slowed, swung off and wheeled forwards. He slid the bike to the ground, reached up and into the hole. His hand closed around a cylinder that yielded a little when squeezed, that had a familiar feel to his fingertips; finely ridged, waxy, slightly slippy but dry. He withdrew and held a fat roll of twenty-pound notes. Philip looked around him. There was no one in sight. He moved over to the bike, placed the money in the panniers at the rear wheel, pushed up the hill, climbed onto the saddle and pedalled hard away.

Philip left the wood, hastened over the footbridge that crossed the river, down the ginnel by the pub and out onto the lane that passed the disused sewage works. At the abandoned tram yard he looked up at the shattered clock face. He turned onto a beaten path that ran close by the railway yard for half a mile or so before turning onto a long, stranded section of the medieval city wall. A steep climb up a bank by a flint-faced tower led out onto a shabby cul-de-sac and past a grubby pub, already open for business. He turned onto the gritted pavement of the main road. The way was empty of people and he put on speed. A minute later Philip stood alone in the unpacking room of the bookshop where he worked, turning the money over and over in his hands.

He cleared a space on the bench, took a red elastic band off the roll and stacked the notes in piles of ten as neatly as he could, though they sprang back as he slapped them down. When he had finished, there were forty stacks and two notes left over. There was more money than he had made in the last year, nearly. More money than he had seen in one place ever, definitely.

He was gathering the notes together when he stopped, walked out onto the shop floor and took a squat, pink pen from under the nearest counter. As he turned he could see Ben, the shop manager, fiddling with his keys at the front shutter. Philip dodged into the unpacking room and drew a line across a few randomly selected notes. They were real. Or real enough. He placed the money back in the pannier, zipped it around and clipped the top shut.

The door swung open and Ben's head popped through.

'Kettle's on.'

He disappeared and a moment later reappeared.

'Morning.'

Philip looked up to say 'right', or something similar, but Ben had gone again. He slumped into a dirty armchair in the corner next to a pile of rejected book returns and ran his hands through his hair again and again. What was he going to do? He couldn't just turn up at the bank with the money. Not all of it. Not eight grand. He couldn't think. *What do they do anyway? Call the police? The Revenue?* He'd put a grand in his bank account and open a new one at a building society. Maybe they wouldn't notice. What would his story be? His aunt had died and left him the money. She didn't trust banks and kept her savings in a shoebox on top of the wardrobe. Did old people still do that? Did it matter?

At lunch time he put the money in a plastic bag, placed it inside another plastic bag and went out. Philip stood outside the building society for a time feeling the weight of the bag on his fingers. He took hold of himself and walked in, a little too quickly, and, without intending, stalked past the long line of people waiting.

'Queue much?' said a woman behind him.

Philip turned around and walked straight out and up the street feeling sick and dizzy. He stopped at the next building society. There was no queue here. The carpet was a dirty powder blue, frayed around the edges. The strip lighting fizzed audibly. He walked up to the counter and the lone tiller looked up and smiled. It was Clarice. A girl he had known at school. A woman, now.

'Hello, you,' she said.

'I want to buy a house ... open an account. Hello ...', he said, 'Hello.'

'Should we try one thing at a time, Philip? In the right order? Shall we start with an account? There are forms on the spinner behind you. I can help you fill one in, if you like. You will need £100 to open an account.'

'I've got this,' he said, and placed the bag on the counter.

'Right.'

She opened the security window and pulled across the money. Philip filled out the form. Clarice reached into the bag, took out the notes and fed them into the cash counter, which flipped and stuttered for a few seconds.

'This is a lot of money, Philip. Do you have any ID?'

'Yes,' he said.

'On you?'

'No.'

'Well, because it's you, I can set everything up and activate the account when you come back with your ID. Two bills with your address on and a form of picture identification. Is that all right? Can you come back later with your ID?'

Philip nodded. Clarice had always talked to him like this, with slow deliberation. He had noticed that he was the only person she spoke to that way.

'We close at 5.30.'

'Can I come back tomorrow?'

'With your ID? At ten o'clock?'

'At ten o'clock ... I'm going now.'

The next day Philip cycled down the path and turned into the wood. He plunged down the dip. A stiff wind had blown up stirring the trees all around. Philip stood in front of the yew. Every branch, each twig, was perfectly still. He reached into the tree and pulled out a large roll of money. The wind grew stronger. The wood seethed and fitted. Philip felt light and permanent, slightly elated, a perfection of calm and clarity at a point of stillness. The sky went black, he closed his eyes and saw a large, dissolving moon. The ground hissed around him. He looked down at his feet buried in copper leaves.

Philip packed the money away and set off, the gale behind him all the way into town.

Philip looked at his workbench. There were eighty stacks of ten twenty-pound notes and two left over.

He touched his head but could feel nothing. There was a thud and a clang at the door. He dived at the money, swept it off the bench and into a box of peanut-shaped packing chips, which tipped over and scattered onto the floor. A woman came in pushing an empty book trolley, talking.

'Promo stock in yet?'

'No ... What? The prize one or the New Year one?

She looked at him a little cross-eyed, pulled up her leggings at the waist and snapped the elastic. Her gaze wandered to the coloured fairy lights that were strung around the steel shelving at the back of the room.

'The prize one?'

'Yes ... No ... It's due in this morning.'

He edged backwards to block her sightline. Should she have one.

'Have you read it?'

'Yeah. It's shit ... Later.'

Philip quickly bagged the money, took the prize-winner from under the bench where he had stored it the evening before, and placed it on the trolley.

He sat in the armchair and waited.

Would the money mean time? What would he do with time? More time? There was the bigger question, the one he had been trying to avoid: where had the money come from? Or rather: where did the money keep coming from? Money had appeared in the tree and, despite having been taken by him, had appeared again. Someone knew and didn't care, or cared but kept doing it anyway. Or were bothered – angered – and had started on a course of reparation, of punishment, that he didn't yet know about. Or perhaps a benefactor was placing the money there. A stranger who had picked Philip out of the deserving, the undeserving, crowd, on whom to confer an unearned gift. It was Clarice. She was stealing from the building society and giving him the money and, by coincidence, he had gone to her to deposit his gains. But how could she know that it would be him that would find the money? She couldn't know. She wouldn't steal from work. It couldn't be Clarice.

Maybe there wasn't a someone, only the money. Somehow, only the money.

Philip pushed the trolley to the front of the shop and left with a large carrier bag.

Clarice pulled the ID through the tray and tapped at her keyboard. She pushed the papers back over with an account 'welcome pack'.

'Welcome,' she said.

Philip stared at her. She looked back at him saying nothing more.

'There's this too,' he said and placed the bag on the counter.

Clarice left her station and reappeared at Philip's side. He looked down at her, felt heavier and, yet, less present, unsure of the self inside, the person noticing him standing here, thinking wordlessly beside Clarice; a much more certain presence than he was, than he could be.

Clarice took the bag and returned behind the glass. She brought up his details, counted and entered the deposit and secured it in a drawer. She pressed a button under the counter next to her knees. She printed out a receipt and slid it across to him. Philip stood still and stared at the receipt. A tall, muscular, bald-headed man appeared behind Clarice and looked out sharp-eyed at Philip, the guard's bottom lip was pulled down revealing a row of stumpy yellow teeth. He tugged his tight suit jacket down and rolled his shoulders.

'I'm over my drawer limit,' said Clarice behind her. 'Goodbye, Philip. Don't forget your receipt.' And she gave a little hand wave from the middle of her chest where her identity badge hung.

Philip stood in front of the tree. Philip stood at his bench counting the money. Philip stood at the counter with four large carrier bags of money. Clarice looked at him, her face signalling something that he could not read. She pressed a few keys on her keyboard and wrote rapidly on a piece of paper.

'Your balance, sir. You can check it more conveniently at the ATM outside or online, if you prefer.' Philip took the note and looked up. She mouthed some words. He smiled at her. She mouthed them again. The words, he realised, were: 'Off you go.'

With the bags at his feet, he sheltered from the rain in the doorway of the closed-down sweet shop up the street and read:

Had to talk my manager out of filing an SAR (big trouble). You need proof of income to avoid being investigated for money laundering. Payslips etc showing bonuses etc. A solicitor's letter detailing bequests. Kind of thing. You can deposit <5k at a time without raising suspicion on the day but if deposits exceed 15k over what you'd usually put in they'll spot it eventually and report you. Destroy this note, please. Do it now.

Each of the next three days Philip returned to the yew tree. On the third day there was as much money as he could fit into both panniers and his backpack. He cycled back home and dropped the day's haul into the bath with the rest of the money. There was enough to buy a small house on the better side of the city. There was enough to buy a large house out in the middle of the fens or on the wild coast. He could sit in front of his fire and grow strange where no one would notice. Go for long, unmeaning walks and open himself out under the sky. The sky would always be bigger than anything his mind could contain. Even the sky itself.

    Philip walked outside. He was late for work. The temperature had fallen several degrees in the short time it had taken him to dump the cash. A clotted grey light hovered close above. Snow began to fall, and so heavily that the going was thick by the time he reached the village. Philip avoided the wood and took the pavements all the way into the city.

    When Philip arrived at the bookshop Ben was standing in the unpacking room looking troubled.

There had been a large delivery of boxes marked 'UR-GENT: NEXT DAY' to add to yesterday's pile. And the stack from the day before.

'Sorry, I'm ... I'll ...'

Ben turned away, stroked his beard and walked through the swing-door onto the shop floor that was already dense with shoppers.

Philip worked steadily, unpacking and checking box after box and pushing the loaded trolleys onto the shop floor. The customers bought the books before the staff managed to get them onto the shelves. The late-opening closing time came and went and he worked on. Ben finished cashing-up and securing the takings. He came into the unpacking room as Philip flattened the last of the unpacked boxes.

'Great day,' said Ben.

'Money?'

'Much money. Should we go?'

The alarm set, Ben unlocked and opened the goods door. There was snow above knee height. More fell steadily.

'The most snow since 1892. And that was by six o'clock. Are you going to be all right getting home?'

'I don't know. Probably.'

'OK. See you tomorrow. There'll likely be no deliveries but come in if you can. Thanks for today, by the way. Cheers.'

Philip walked round the corner into the market square. The city was white and soundless. The church, venerable and dark-windowed, illuminated from all sides, appeared weightless, more massive than its modern neighbours. He stopped before the statue of the doctor-philosopher seated in contemplation. As he did each time he came by, Philip read the blackened plaque beneath: *We carry with us the wonders.*

The snow was too deep and soft for cycling but he had no trouble in making progress on foot. He turned left by the ruined abbey, cut through the scrubby woods above the car park and headed towards the tower. Philip reached the main road near the swing bridge. A burger van, with no lights on, slid down the road sideways and came to a halt. A woman in a housecoat and headscarf stepped out and, without closing the passenger door, walked unsteadily but rapidly up to a dark row of terraced houses. A door opened, a hand reached out and pulled her in.

Philip crossed and followed the river until he could no longer. He took the path past the works towards the village but before arriving at the street he turned into the long meadow. He passed over the lane into the woods. The snow was lighter on the ground despite the leaf fall. The quiet was more complete. The ticking of the bike seemed louder, an imposition on the dark. Philip took hold of the frame and swung it around his shoulder. He approached the dip and hesitated. In the distance a rushing sound began that he could not identify. It had a harsher quality than the descending snow, more white noise than falling ice. He ran down the incline towards the yew tree, feet juddering in his boots. He lowered the bike to the ground and approached.

Through the trees the noise grew louder. Philip felt warmth on his back. He turned and saw a wavering line of pale yellow at the edge of the wood. A thump and a rustle and a fox appeared with scores of skittering mice at its feet. A dozen large grey rats arrived and ran back and forth in circles around the fox. A stoat jittered past, something bloody sagging in its mouth.

Over the ridge past the tree, to his left and right, on all sides, light, orange light, advanced. Heat rose rapidly through the seasons to summer. Hot high summer. Philip wanted to undress, to drink lemonade, to lie down. He sensed diffuse movement ahead.

A vast bustling of feathery beats burst through the air. A dark cloud of thrushes, wrens, blackbirds. Philip crouched and covered his face with his coat. Birds battered him for a long minute. He stood, shook off some feathers and turned to the tree. He stepped forward, placed his hand in the hollow, groped around inside and felt nothing but a small soft nub at the base of the cavity. He pinched gently with his thumb and forefinger and brought the object out. A large, still, black moth; uncrushed. The fire was in a circle no more than thirty feet away from him, closing in quickly on every side. The moth twitched and he let go. The creature's black satiny wings pulled it up towards the red sky. Philip watched its flight to the crown of the tree. A heron stood gazing down at him, its great white wings open, unmoving. Philip embraced the tree and pressed his cheek to the cool bark. The fire surged around. He held on harder and called out of his dry mouth.

'Come in you wonders … All you wonders … Come on.'

Philip released the tree and stepped back. He looked up through tatters of smoke into the starlight, found a foothold and began to climb.

WONDER MEADOW

The night trees were blue by the Wensum. Eels seethed in a ditch. In the flint wall of a garden a door trembled. A green man sat naked on the riverbank, his feet in the water, head nodding, vines and tendrils ran down his chest. A swan guzzled between his legs, blood flowed down his mossy thighs. Burning ropes suspended from the boughs of a hawthorn tree, twitching and jiggling. Across a playing field the cathedral rose, all spire, dissolving sour yellow into the sky, drifting towards the moon.

Cakes were scattered in the mud by the Watergate. The girl guides were elsewhere, in bed. The guides carers' were in bed also. Or sitting at a kitchen table with a mug of malted milk staring at their reflection in the black glass of a garden door.

A walking stick, made from a shark's backbone, floated down the river. A leprous-white hand attached. And to the hand, an arm, a body. Lids flickered, eyes opened; large, luminous green. The man was a watcher. Watching himself looking out for others to whom he could attach his gaze.

Andrea tucked the hospital gown into the waistband of her jeans. She sang a song of her own making. She smiled, which made her think of teeth, her teeth, and she smiled again, broader this time. A plaster covered the puncture mark in her left hand. The hand was sore and a number of the fingers numb at their tips. She stopped and looked at her hand, fearing, for a moment, that it would become another thing, shears or claws or jaws, or another's. Another's perfect hand, unscarred, cold and steady with silver fingernails and dry palms. Andrea wanted to be sure that she would not change any more than was necessary.

Men came down the path. Three men. One stared, eyes out of his head. One sang and leered. One walked with a swinging stride, hands in pockets, his face two tiny eyes, a red gash of wet lips. Three men taking possession of the night.

Andrea knew the moment they noticed her from the thickening of the air in her throat, from the return of pain to her left shoulder, from the sudden heaviness of her boots, the stickiness of their soles. The men called. They told her what they thought she was. They told her what they wanted to do. They told her what they were going to do.

Andrea stood still in the middle of the path. The river slowed and stopped. The river speeded up. The men came closer, growing smaller all the while. Andrea reached into the gown pocket and took out a gross anatomy knife. The men came on, their sounds more distant, their forms shrinking away. The handle was plastic, lemon yellow and warm. Andrea drew long lines where they might have been. The air parted with a sucking sound, again and again. The men whispered in the grass, they had not passed but they were gone.

She tossed the knife into the river, wet before it hit the water, picked up her tune and followed the way towards the road. The trees shivered as she passed. Canaries with glass beaks fussed and chittered in the air a few feet above and behind. Andrea reached in her pocket and found the knife. Safe.

Wavering orange light was visible through the trees, cries drifted with the smoke from Lollards Pit across the river. The path warped to her left, ran through a wicket, past a cottage and out before a tower. The Cow Tower. The place she would meet her friend Judith. Andrea walked on but could not see her. She passed round the tower to a tall iron gate and looked through. On a green silk divan reclined a large woman in a great fur coat.

'Aren't you terrible hot, Judy?'

'I like to be cosy, don't you know, old girl. You're looking less than marvellous, if I might say. You made it here all right?'

'A little local difficulty. Nothing to speak of, darling. How did you get in there?'

'The ladies from the Adam and Eve carried me over. Would you believe it? Big girls the lot of them. My kind.'

Judith reached over and switched on a tall standard lamp. Yellow light projected upwards, illuminating the canaries that swirled above where the upper floors used to be, making their beaks sparkle.

'How should I...'

'Just give a good firm shove, love.'

The gate moved, shifting a mound of dried leaves forward with a hush. Andrea looked up and around.

A dark circle of blue, the sky, a ring of gun ports, another of arrow loops, pellitory and red valerian grew in effusions on every welcoming surface.

'The armchair is for you, sweetie. You must be exhausted after your troubles. No one was less deserving of troubles than you, dearest. Curse the deserving, the bastards.'

'You wouldn't have a cup of tea, would you?'

'Haven't I flask? And a hamper too? You're starved, of course.'

Andrea took a melamine willow-pattern plate out of the basket and raided the same for gala pie, potato salad with chives, for asparagus spears sopping with butter, for sweet tomato chutney, for a salad of endives, marigold leaves, watercress and sorrel soured with vinegar. She was a long time eating and all the while Judith watched her contentedly, pulling from time to time on the pipe of a port sipper glass. Andrea poured herself a mug of tea and settled back in the armchair.

'Did you tell them at the hospital before you left? That you were going to leave?'

'I did not.'

'Might they look for you?'

'I suppose they might. But I'm here aren't I? Where they aren't. And I haven't done anything wrong.'

'You haven't done anything wrong.'

'I haven't done anything wrong.'

'You haven't done anything wrong.'

Andrea took a fat gulp of tea.

'Have I done something wrong, Judy?'

'You haven't done anything wrong, my love. Not a thing.'

'Only to myself.'

'Only to yourself.'

'What did I do that for Judy?'

'You know why, honeybear.'

'I can take care of myself now.'

'You should.'

'Do you love me, Judy?'

'I do.'

Judith patted the silk heavily raising a small cloud of dust out of the horsehair. Andrea dropped the mug and rose, the plate fell on the stones, she approached the sofa, Judith opened her coat and her arms and embraced Andrea, enfolding her, pulling her close, stroking her hair. As Andrea began to fall asleep Judith reached out and turned off the lamp. Judith could feel the knife through the gown.

Andrea woke, blinking, alone on the divan, swaddled in fur. Six girls in brown and yellow uniforms crowded around the gate, gazing down at her, their faces bright, shiny and serious.

'She's awake.'

'We can *see* that...'

'Would you like a cake, lady?'

'Shutup...'

All but one of the girls laughed. The one who offered the cake.

'Cake for breakfast?' said Andrea.

The girls danced, singing: 'Cake for breakfast! Cake for breakfast!'

Andrea walked, smiling, to the gate. The unsmiling girl pressed an open pink toffee tin forward, crowded with fairy cakes, each topped with a thick, vermicular swirl of buttercream and a scattering of blue and yellow sugar stars.

'Take one...'

Andrea took one.

'Take another.'

She took another.

'Thank you,' said Andrea.

'Bye! Bye!' said five of the girls, and they skipped off.

The unsmiler stood still. She returned the lid to the tin.

'We're picking up rubbish today. Along the river.'

'Oh...that sounds...'

The girl interrupted her with a solar, yellow-toothed smile. She held the cake tin up at a distance from her uniform and marched away.

Andrea shuffled off the fur. She stood looking up to the new sun and raised an arm to protect her face from a shower of hard bright objects; birdless glass beaks. Andrea squeezed through the narrow gate gap, turned back to the river. She walked down Ferry Lane towards Tombland. A lone horse passed by slowly, pulling an empty cart. In the shadowed window of a house was a rocking horse with a mouth too large for its head and ivory slabs for teeth, as if it had not quite finished eating a piano. The lane sank and river water flowed rapidly along the deep channel. Andrea stepped to one side and a large boat with a tall mast under a single sail came on, one man fore and another aft, throwing, pushing and pulling on long poles. Roped together on deck were two vast pieces of roughly dressed, creamy limestone. The water flowed back to the river and the channel filled in.

Andrea stopped next to a gate in a black iron fence. A sign read: Browne's Meadow. She stepped in and onto the large bituminous rectangle of a car park bounded by red brick walls and, beyond these, by willows and sallows that nodded and soughed in a soft breeze. A fine, many-handed chestnut roan stood at the centre, its haunches facing her, its tail flicked as she approached. She made a wide circle round to face the horse, which she patted and then embraced around the neck. The ground became soft under her soles. The cars were sheep. The tarmac was grass and sweet briar, bramble and mulberry, whortle-berry and holly, juniper and gorse, cornelian and hazel; bilberries, redcurrants, gooseberries, dog's mercury, barberries and bittersweet grew in random profusion. Andrea released the horse's head and it plodded into the distance.

Andrea sat in the wonder meadow. She felt the similitude of her limbs to the various parts of nature surrounding and thought of how she might be joined to them more completely, more fruitfully. Her skin was bark to her. Her body south-facing always, a spirit searching for union, for extension, for vegetable tranquillity, unpractised in green ways, in rootedness, but sapful, exalted and germinal. She might, with the aid of an artful incision, grow atop a hawthorn, or an alder, an oak or a hawthorn, or entwine herself for life within a gorse bush, a thousand shining yellow eyes, spiny green fingers, tough branched arms, scenting the air by day and night.

Memory is an arsonist, setting fires cell-deep at ungovernable intervals of time and space. Lights go on, searching out pain. The hands of another. The mother voice, singing to block out the noise. Titanic laughter and with it confusion. Clouds, white, grey striations, disposed across the eye. The folded heron in the reed bed, the river drifting deeply, its world mirroring still. Judy sat on the orange plastic seats in casualty. And again, Judy waiting on the orange plastic seats in casualty. And later, Judy waiting on the green plastic seating in casualty. For Andrea to return, clean and swathed.

It might be the deep chill damp of the earth rising or her body warmth sinking into the meadow but there is a gradual cooling, a dimming, an extinguishing. For the first time since memory began these hard fires, their successions, their wasting, their consummations, their miseries, go down and out and mindsmoke drifts, drifts away. The dark, at last, is light.

The suffering blue of the sky called her back from the green, the hard tar and grit beneath her gown; a sheep, a car, beeping its horn.

Andrea stood and brushed herself down. The driver spoke some sour words out of their window and reversed to park. Out in the lane Andrea headed for the cathedral close through a crowd of grinning blue-uniformed boys. She sat on a bench and looked up at the pink-tinged spire, at a falcon stood distantly on the air aside its uppermost taper.

'When I rise,' she said. 'I shall be free.'

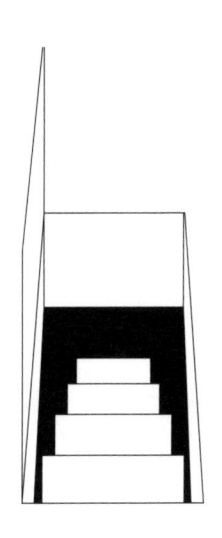

Eley Williams

Tether

There was a white balloon and a strange man in my garden, neither one tethered to the other. The moon was as bright and silly as you might expect.

During the evening I thought the air felt charged as if squaring up for rain or something more pushy. Once the indigos and sky-threads of apricot and pink had tidied themselves away, smoothed and patted down their corners beneath the line of the garden fence, I made sure to stare directly at the moon in case it got any funny ideas. I did not expect a man and a balloon to be there on the patio beneath my window.

I did not look directly at the balloon for fear of bursting it and did not want to look at the man for fear of fear so I moved to the centre of my window and glared at the moon instead, treating it as a balloon-by-proxy and ambassador for the man.

'Please leave my garden,' I mouthed behind my glass. It misted over so that the words could not reach the garden. Moon, balloon and man were ridiculous and littering my evening. I rubbed my breath's condensation from the window and momentarily gave the moon new contours with my thumbprint.

Vaguely aware that the balloon was nudging along my garden's back wall, only just skimming the surface of the patio and moving away from the unmoving man, I faced the moon head-on and narrowed my eyes. It changed shape against the dark as I squinted – its dot become a dollop and then a mere dash above the clouds. All of the white stars and the yellow street lamp across the road shifted too so that their dots became dollops became dashes of light, tessellating and fusing until my eyes were shut and the dark was soft.

The word *dollop* has a pleasing twist of internal symmetry when written down in a recipe. I imagine that if you ladled some moon into a hot pan for a moment there would be a flattened amount of liquid in the spoon's bowl and a column of moon suspended between the ladle and freshly poured disc of moon on the pan's surface. Two moon-pools tethered together mid-dollop with the shape of that pour, its architecture, possessesing a kind of symmetry too. I am glad that the moon is not lopsided. If it was, who could ever trust a sky again? I can't remember the time I last ate.

I opened one of my eyes. The man was still standing in my garden. He seemed unaware of the balloon. I hope he did not think I was winking at him.

I am not a good gardener. Some days I wonder if it would be better to say that I attend to the needs of aphids in new and exciting ways. Plants seem to blanch and die quicker in my garden than in my neighbours'. I listen to all the Top Tips on the gardening programmes, I order the hardiest perennials, browse for the most efficient-but-ethical pesticides and make sure to water everything regularly according to taste and need. The soil I buy online is expensive and feels good between my hands but flowers and plants shrivel here far faster than I would expect. Shrubs' leaves become riddled and splayed, buds bow their heads and fold their chins against their chests in premature defeat. The beans I trained died and left me with only their little wicker teepees draped in brown hollowed stalks. They looked rusty somehow. I grew plants so that there would be words like *lush* and *verdant* and *herbaceous* in my garden through my window but now it's all *skeletal* and *chitinous* and *patio slabs*.

Is the man also looking at moon? Is my garden the best spot in the world for moon-watching?

The white balloon came to a stop in the corner of my yard beneath one of the birdfeeders. I keep birdfeeders filled with seeds – children of plants too soon for this world, delivered to my door in bags of glossy full stops and apostrophes. The feeders' visitors mean that there is at least occasional colour outside my window with the robins and the blue tits and the quiffy, spiffy chaffinches queuing up to eat on the plastic perches. The goldfinches are particularly welcome as are the wood pigeons who know the difference between *dove* and *dived*. A pair of goldfinches have taken to swinging on one of the feeders in the centre of the patio, getting their heads right against the plastic column of it in order to gain access to the seeds. That might be their first and only experience of touching of plastic, I think. Their swinging action knocks a number of the feeders' grain to the ground where the wood pigeons are waiting. Even from up here behind my window I can hear the pigeons mumbling contentedly in their throats as they waddle about as seeds fall about their feet as the goldfinches set about their work. I rap on the window pane whenever a squirrel attempts to muscle-in on this relationship but my heart's not really in it. On the whole this year I have found that squirrels, goldfinches, pigeons and moons ignore me. I prefer it this way.

A siren dopplered some roads away, like sound was rolling way from its own grasp.

I think the man is smelling the single white rose by my fence.

As I say, mine is not much of a garden and I am not much of a gardener but one rose had done something like survive this year. It had a small bloom, smaller than a fist and the colour of cheap ice-cream. Already I suspected I could see an unhealthy tinge and crease at the larger petals' extremities but it was a bonny thing to catch sight of through my window. I fed it cups of bone meal which never sounded right, yet!, here it was, smelling of vanilla and bergamot and Christmas and childhoods' laundries. I imagined that perhaps this man had passed by my garden, felt the air glitch and fizz with the smell of this single rose in the night, and simply had to investigate. Who knows where he had come from – maybe he had smelled it from miles away, a faint tang or tangle, snagging of scent on the breeze and he had made it his mission to seek out the source. I imagined him vaulting over hedgerows in the dark, nostrils flared as he dodged traffic and dog-walkers. He might have closed his eyes and decided to trust only his nose as he scrambled over suburban street signs and kerbsides and parking metres. I had not left my house or garden for over a year so must admit I was not too sure of the hazards beyond what I could see from my window. It's not that I'm scared, it just feels safer within the bounds of my fence. I would not want to deny anyone a smell of this single rose. I am proud of it, after all, and it's not like he's going to drain it of its scent however hard he breathes it in. I look at the man looking at my rose and, although he should not be here, there is a sudden fellow-feeling.

The balloon is another matter. It might snag on the rose's thorns and burst, waking the neighbours or any roosting goldfinches or woodpigeons or aphids. Its deflated white puckered nonsense of a body would then be latched on the rose's stem and the former balloon, littering even as it littles itself, would be using the rose as a mere prop.

I read an article once in a library, back when I could leave my house and garden. It was by an Apollo 17 astronaut who claimed the moon smelled like gunpowder.

Did the man perhaps bring the balloon? It is white to match the rose – is this his idea of an exchange or expression of thanks? It is surely no coincidence that they both arrived at the same time in my deadening garden unless my patio is about to play host to an influx of unrelated objects. The balloon was scudding along the ground in such a way that one can assume it was filled with breath rather than helium. He is a large man, I think. He looks large enough to fill a balloon with just a few breaths: it would not be so great a gift

– thoughtful but not too costly. I wonder if this man's breath might be heavier than mine. He may breathe in great dollops. My breath feels very slight and thin and barely mists a window pane, even when I'm so close to it.

'Is it your balloon?' I mouthed to the window and my breath doesn't even register this time, no flare of frost appearing against its surface.

The man looked up. He stared right at me in the window. It is obvious he is not smelling my rose and that he has not brought it a balloon to barter for its scent. He is showing he can not only leave his house but also walk down any road he chooses, open any gate he wants, stand in any garden he desires and refuse to smell even its most brilliant flowers.

I am at the threshold of my bedroom door, I am at the top of the stairs, I am one hand on the latch then the chain, then the handle of the door and I am in the garden. The patio is cold against my feet and I feel old unpigeoned birdseed beneath my soles.

'This is mine,' I say, not looking at the man. I mean the garden and I mean it firmly but I am reaching for the balloon as the words escape me.

'Is this yours?' I say, asking the balloon. I take it in both hands so that I am sure it will not slip away. I feel certain somehow that it will make a run for it, bob up and away and nudge its cousin moon in the ribs, laughing squeakily at my inability to leave my bad garden and my unmistable house.

It is lighter in my hands than I expected.

'What are you doing,' I say to myself as I try and twist the balloon, to pierce its skin with my nails. I had a sudden notion that I wanted to flatten it or roll it into a tight, light ball and throw it at the man. Its shape will not budge or squash at all between my thumbs, however. If anything it almost feels like it swells a little.

The man does not move but makes a sniffing sound. I hope he is irritated that I am ignoring him. I can smell the rose from here, its vanilla and laundry and clean hopefulness opening the night in half to let something good in. Why is he here, the smell of the rose seems to say, littering or loitering or opening your garden gate if not to tell me how perfect your rose is or the light of the moon might be? Does he think he should hop over any door just because he can? How many gardens and spaces and places has he taken up during this whole year that I have sat by my window counting the goldfinches and the falling seeds, ordering more seeds once the feeders are empty?

I cannot seem to gain purchase on the balloon and I want to stamp on it, see it flat beneath my feet and darkened in the soil and dust and dirt of my garden. It strikes me that I have not eaten all day and I am drunk on the braveness of the smell of the despite-everything-rose and I think that if I cannot burst this hideous balloon between my fingernails that I will bite it, and so I do, I take the smallest nip at the part of the balloon nearest its knot, its neck.

There is no bang and nothing monstrous. I am holding a flat cold sigh in my hands. The balloon does not look slumped nor dead, just a wrinkled useless thing in my hands. As I broke its surface with my teeth perhaps it was my imagination but I felt a fleeting new not-coolness play against my face as someone else's breath escaped and thickened the air. That breath smelt of nothing at all.

I faced the man standing uninvited and strange in my garden, a broken balloon and freed breath between us in the rose-stink and the yellow lamp light. The moon leaned in, perhaps, amongst the unsquinted stars.

It was too dark to make out any of the man's features but I could see well enough to know that he was smiling. I watched him take a step back away from me, towards the garden gate. I held the breathless balloon to him the very moment that he angled his head slightly to one side, loosened his jaw, took the whole head of the white rose in his mouth and gently bit right down through its stem.

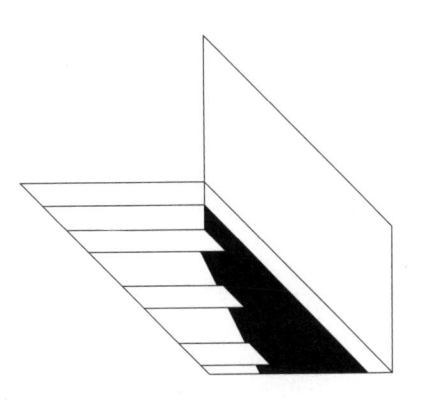

Lily Hackett

Two Fictions

GIRLS' HOLIDAY

We are girls and we are going on a holiday which makes it, even to a skeptic, or someone with an axe to grind, or a nose to shove in the mud, a girls' holiday.
  When you think of our holiday, think of cool white galleries. Sunburned legs and silence. I honestly think it would be better for you to imagine us all the same.
  We play a strip game. Michael is quite chubby but with a large penis so takes off his trousers first, and Dion is quite muscular but with a smallish one, so takes off his top first. Our holiday is not white and cool at all, but smells of a four-day fly buffet, of ass and gas and ash.
  On the outskirts is a club. Some nights they hold a fetish-style night that includes being whipped on your way in. I must insist on my individual experience of this night, despite the fact that we all find German boys to tongue into the morning. I write mine something carefully wrought. He writes back something careless and happy.
  There is a show that plays: people, couples, bid on the contents of shipping containers. Sometimes they contain photos of people dying of cancer, but, if you are lucky, sometimes they don't. One girl dances better than all of us girls, in the same way that some shipping containers now contain pop-up shops and cafes, and some still contain dead people's things.
  On our holiday there are no squares, only straight lines, but each line leads your eye to a circle. Imagine

four girls in a gallery, but multiply them, so that whatever room you walk into, there is a lovely schoolgirl going crisp at the shoulders, looking at a painting called The Sun Eater. What is notable about this painting is that even though the sun eater is massive, and can easily fit the sun inside its body, it looks like it has regretted the decision.

There is a song that plays: the song says in it that there is never going to be enough space.

THE PITY OF SCALE

There is a story. A man in the story talks about a story he read in the news. A woman has sex while high on crack, and then gives birth, straight into the toilet. She does not take the baby out of the toilet, but goes back to the man in the story. The man says in the story, about this story, *I understood I was reading a story about the end of mankind.*

Here is the same sort of story. A woman approaches a house at night. The house is not hers, but she knows its geometry. She does not slip on the steep front step, does not bash her brains in on the concrete path, though this is a story with death in its belly. She has been drinking cider flavoured with black and purple fruits, staining her lips, almost like red wine, but darker and bluer, like she has sucked the ink up from a pen. She opens the door with the key she was given a while ago for a specific reason.

Inside she sinks into a pink sofa, the kind that both submits to a body and forces a body to submit. It will be hard for her to get back up. She is the wrong sort of drunk. There are right sorts. Her big fists are out because they want to give something a squeeze. She finds she cannot stay on the sofa, and paces around, opening and closing her fists.

There are two snakes on the floor of the room. The woman looks down at the snakes. Now the woman is in the kitchen. Inside the fridge are two mice in a packet. It is not sadness the woman feels, but the pity of scale: they are small and she is not. Her fists squeeze the packet until there is blood inside the plastic. She closes the fridge, picks up a pair of scissors printed with leopard print on the blades. She is back in the snake room now, with her bloody clutch of mousey bits.

She takes the first snake, holds its head hard under her thumb, holds out her arm so that the snake cannot coil around her neck. She takes the scissors to the place on the snake that on anything else would be a throat.

The scissors are open so wide that the blades make a single straight line. Cutting the snake feels like cutting through rope, or raw chicken breast, or like cutting into her arm. She takes the second snake, does it again. The scissors scrape and slip on the scales, making the scales flake onto her fingers. She licks them off, sucks them up, licks her lips, thinks: *there is less blood than I thought there would be.*

The woman looks down at the floor, down at the four pieces of snake. Now that the tails are off, they look a lot like the mice in the packet: slim heads, smart eyes, small now and throatless.

She puts the first snake's head in her mouth. The snake tastes like coins, feels like coins too. It is too big for her mouth, so she gags. She puts the second head in her mouth. It tastes like coins, feels like coins, sounds like coins as she bites down: like coins in a coin game in an arcade, a stack of coins scaling a ledge.

This is how her sister finds her: as with all terrible things, there is surprisingly little screaming.

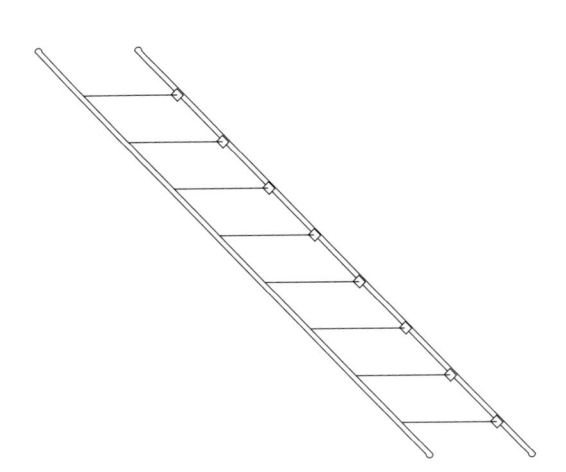

Brian Evenson

A Report on Translation

In her book on hotels, W. quotes F. on genitalia: 'I give both organs and processes their technical names... I call a spade a spade.' F., who was Austrian, did not actually call a spade a spade. Nor did he choose to employ German and call a *Spaten* a *Spaten*. Instead, resorting to French, the language of diplomacy, F. actually said '*J'appelle un chat un chat*' ('I call a cat a cat.') In the English translation, animal has become implement.

The philosopher G. points out that only rarely is a cat just a cat, since *chat or chatte can be used as a vulgar (vulvar) slang for the female genitalia*. Saying you call a cat a cat is not as straightforward or innuendo-less as it might seem.

F. is better known for having said 'sometimes a cigar is just a cigar,' though he doesn't seem to have actually said this either – nor said anything equivalent to it in either German or French. As E. suggests, *not only do we lack any written record of F. as the direct source, but also there are many reasons to conclude that F. never said it or anything like it*. But someone said F. said it, and now everybody believes F. did.

Cats and spades, spades and cats. Spayed cats. Surely F.'s English translator must have been aware of what he was doing, moving from a word, '*chat*,' that hints at female genitalia, to a word that sounds like a term for sterilizing animals. It's even better, though, if it's a kind of slip, of the kind that F. popularized and that takes his name: a misstatement that uncovers a hidden truth.

Though, in fact, F. never used the word 'slip' either. Nor did he use the word 'parapraxis,' the Greek word his English translator used in place of his German word, *Fehlleistungen*'. His word is better translated as 'faulty actions' or 'misperformances.'

Which, in the end, is exactly what translation is: a series of faulty actions and misperformances, which, nonetheless, at their best, at their most slippery, reveal things that the more correct original might not.

Greg Mulcahy

Slide

Goerske had them meet in a meeting room though no one understood how Goerske had risen to a place that allowed Goerske to call meetings.

Goerske started as though it were a movie where company assembled recalled and then flashed back to the life of the dead one.

Really it is a story of love, Sister in Praise said.

Goerske gave her the look Goerske gave non-persons.

Jesus, he said, could this be more trope tired?

Those tropes, Sister in Praise said, have a reason. A function beyond your understanding.

For a meeting room, the chairs were uncomfortable. But the colors were suitably bland.

He will return, Sister in Praise said, in glory.

I never really, he said, understood what glory meant.

There's not going to be any resurrection, Goerske said. At least not in our time. And probably never.

Who, he said, would scope probability on something like that?

Not a non-person like you, Goerske said.

We see resurrection, Sister in Praise said, every day in the cycle of rebirth.

No, Goerske said. That is not it. The two are not the same, and things are only what they are. Nothing is but what is.

Did anyone, he said, think to order a sandwich tray?

153   *Greg Mulcahy*

This is not a meal, Goerske said.

Well, he said, when he was dying –

Dying, Goerske said, the differ a' the dead.

Losing your speech? He said.

You understand me clear enough, Goerske said.

Goerske started the slides, which were not slides, but were called slides after the slides which were slides.

Anyone familiar with cyclical presentations could have predicted the order.

Sister in Praise wept quietly.

He had a hard time staying awake.

Goerske, reviewing the dead man's life, shaped a narrative that related more to Goerske than the dead man.

There was a solemn portrayal.

And the slides of fun.

A theme of fond memories.

Handed out cards for something called The Society For Greater Alignment though the cards did not indicate what was to be aligned.

It is anger, Sister in Praise said. It is the world false.

Anger at the world true, he said, anger at the world false. Why not just leave it at anger?

What, Goerske said.

Everything, he said. This is a badly addressed envelope anyway.

That is a barely coherent remark, Goerske said. The slides were out of order. Once they are re-ordered, we can begin again at the beginning.

Why don't we, he said, begin again at the end?

There is no end, Sister in Praise said. Everything is never-ending.

The prospect, he said, grimmer than the slides. Or the new beginning.

Everybody take a break, Goerske said. We'll get this put back together.

You couldn't do it the first time, he said.

He went out to the lot.

Nothing was happening in the lot.

When people still smoked, people smoked there. Now people were fat instead.

He knew he was putting on weight.

In the existing or non-existing end, it would all go away.

A banner rustled in the wind.

He knew a time before banners, but he was not sure when the banners arrived.

Or why.

Banner, an ancient icon, now for some reason a contemporary necessity.

Goerske waddled onto the lot.

Goerske, he said, when did they get this banner?

It was, Goerske said, part of the rebrand.

When was that?

Which one?

Whichever brought the banner in.

I don't know, Goerske said.

There was a hierarchy, he said, long time. Seemed like it was always going to be there. Then all that rebranding.

Born to hierarchy granite, Goerske said. Now, not a dream of cassette aired. By the way, you're on the banner.

What's that mean?

Find out, Goerske said. Then figure it out. There has to be a report. A report is expected.

That's a helpful suggestion.

Helpful suggestions have gone by us, Goerske said. They were never helpful anyway.

True, he said.

11

Nobody knew.

Facilities said the banners came from a bannerworks in another state.

Facilities gave him a brochure.

What Banner Raised? the brochure said.

Business in Life, the brochure said.

There was a brief, unhelpful, and probably inaccurate history of banners.

And a list affirming banner uses or potential uses: city halls, schools, businesses, churches, or even streetlights.

Even.

He did not feel even.

He did not feel he was starting even.

It was obvious he was starting at a loss.

Not that Goerske would have it any other way.

Goerske reflexively pressed every advantage, no matter how small or useless.

Damaging even.

Goerske referred to this as Goerske's body of work.

Streetlight – what about a fountain – a fountain surrounded by banners?

He had seen such a thing.

He was sure of it.

Perhaps in the plans.

Perhaps in the mock up.

The new facility with its internationally-designed Garden of Agony.

The focal point.

The whole thing based, if he remembered right, on a famous picture of a famous cathedral in fog.

The fog gray.

The cathedral gray.

But were there not the flaming leaves of Fall against or within the gray?

Those and something about a desire for coherence.

Not that coherence or desire was part of the picture or reflected in the design.

Coherence more a psychological thing.

Difficulty to express visually.

A monument for or against in any case.

Statement of the first day or reflection of the last day.

Both, maybe.

Or the elements of despair – illustrated.

Had to look good in the rain.

That had to be designed into the design.

But anything that would look good in the fog would look good in the rain.

Package in the package of slides for presentation so anyone could see.

A dedicated monument and working facility.

Not exactly a living museum.

Living museum a concept maybe not as popular as it once was.

Problem, maybe, of association.

People saw things that were perhaps not there but that they thought reflected something of their lives.

Something, often as not, unpleasant.

Many busy regretting life stultified.

Or hating any attempt at familiarity.

Problematic for many to understand life as other than a series of betrayals.

Maybe physical.

Mechanical.

Case of damaged polarities or some metaphor similar.

A monument, in a sense, for that.

The monumental focused.

The monument demanding clarity from visitor and denizen alike.

It was clarity, wasn't it?

Always?

At the end?

Though all that far from the slides or presentation or plan.

Presentation had to do with belief.

Not his.

Not even clear.

But some belief all the same.

He was, he thought, engaged in a transaction though the exact nature of the transaction was not yet clear and would only become clear as the transaction progressed, if at all.

He had a tongue in his mouth.

There was a voice in his head.

For now, if he did not slip, that was enough.

Of course there was that slipping desperate.

Or desperate slip away all click and done.

Click.

Now he was in the rain as though he had told himself he would never again in the rain.

The telling, the talk, the slip.

Though he had not told himself anything.

And would not.

Important to leave the talk to those who talk.

Let them phrase the throw-away beautiful.

Goerske and the rest, the ash bureaucrats of central casting.

Cost to it.

Cost to a thing.

Always other interests included.

Kind or varieties of public statement.

Gas dream publicist dreaming himself popular.

Or competent in competence powerful for Goerske.

And there was no escape Goerske.

Or Goerske's ilk.

Ilk more likely the article.

Though ilk as though Goerske a product infinitely reproducible.

A type, one language said.

Language not his.

Tapped out was tapped out.

Goerske or not.

All the Goerskes. As a class. As a horde created.

Lectured him on improvement through grief.

The lesson.

The Inspiration.

What it was to mean to him.

A brochure, Goerske gave him, of grief brochured.

And the banner brochure.

Brochures, it seemed, strongly resilient in the age of electron and slide.

Poor map, still comforting in four-color print and slick graphic.

Tangible as well.

Something for the tangible still.

Or even now.

As in music.

The music with the presentation.

Reinforcing, it seemed, the slides.

Or the song.

Song some guy from there wrote, *Momma never did like me.*

Something like that.

Yet a limit to the music he could allow himself to hear in his head.

Not as though he lived in a work of art though he

had heard some lived that way.
    Lived that as though.
    He had lived in a room with forced heat and convict-pictured walls.
    Well away from that.
    As often any away might be well away.
    Different cracks in the walls and fades in the stair runners.
    Though stair runners, it seemed, were going or had gone out.
    As though some history escaped him.
    But what?
    A history of cheap furnishing?
    And cheaply furnished, what did cheaply furnished care?
    Or care to know?
    He could not dwell forever in the dead furnishings of the past as those furnishings existed now only in the imagination.
    Imagined past the only true past.
    Not as though he had, or it was, something to say.
    Somebody always saying something.
    Somebody.
    Nothing for him to say.
    Or to be said.
    It was maybe time to forget.
    What forget meant.

III

The facility in the distant city.

He flew to it and stayed in the arranged lodging.

Waited.

Called Goerske as he was told to call Goerske if there were a problem.

You wanted, Goerske said, a direct communication?

Goerske talked awhile about the significance of day and date, of vestment and color of garment and symbolic value.

Sister in Praise told me all this, Goerske said. Stay where you are, and you will see.

As though the random made sacred or the sacred proved random.

I'll wait, he said.

Mallou hammered his door. He opened.

I'm Mallou, Mallou said.

I am, he said.

I know, Mallou said. You're the ghost to give me this phantom pain. Let me do what I must. You need a guide. You suffer a lack of guidance. Suppose it has all been arranged. Leave the sequence to me. Remember any sequence is only a progression.

This, Mallou said, is about a banner. Not carpet. Not letterhead. A goal needs a pathway. A pathway needs a structure. A structure needs a map.

Yes, he said.

I must go now, Mallou said. A guide is not a companion.

His teeth hurt.
Payment for the dentist denial payment.
Benefits reduced.
As ever.
Still, could he, at any cost, go to a strange dentist in a strange city?
Not thought to ask Mallou.
He would make a list.
Better, keep a list.
Running list of questions.
He might encounter anything as this – trip – different.
This Banner Pilgrimage assigned.
All and every world going or gone, this would go as well.
List a kind of control.
Questions kinds of markers.
No negotiation in this, merely request.
Nothing negotiable in this.
If there were, he would refuse it as he had lost his desire to negotiate.
Necessary loss, it seemed.
An inventory, Goerske had said.
Of the tools.
Of the objects.
Of the paperwork.
Everything banner or banner-related to be laid out.
He accepted.
Whether he had chosen or not not a meaningful question.

This was not a coast on sleeve or margin.
Though sleeve or margin might be in this.
He was as he understood it to get to the center.
Or the central.
The heart.
As the pictured often-times heart in flames.
Not real flames.
Flames a metaphor for importance or intensity or passion.
Importance, he was sure of that.
To find the importance.
That was it.
You seem, Mallou said, troubled.
I have not, he said, not since all of this, slept well.
How are your dreams?
Dull and tedious in the night. I dreamed someone stole the trashcan from in front of my house. I labored mightily to recover or replace it, but could not.
Yes, Mallou said, that is it. The gristle dream. The trivial agony of daily obligation. This is your experience.
Mallou gave him a pamphlet.
The pamphlet entitled *A Strange Tale*.
Study this, Mallou said.
Mallou left him in the reading room.
He began.

A Strange Tale
The dog spoke often of his early days in the forest, running in packs, hunting whatever the pack gave chase, happily following the alpha's lead.

What, the man said, are you called, dog?

Barks Kincaid, the dog said.

The man was not certain. The dog spoke clearly in a pleasant voice, but the man was not convinced the dog actually spoke. The man thought perhaps the dog could not speak and the whole thing was an illusion using the recorded voice of an actor or perhaps some kind of computer technology.

Go to the warehouse, Barks Kincaid said, and expect the treasure which has been laid there. You will see what the orderly arrangement of objects can offer.

And you, the man said, will you come with me and act as my guide?

You need no guide, Barks Kincaid said. The warehouse is well known to you.

At the warehouse, there were no packages. Instead, the man saw his father there. He had not seen his father in many years, not since his father died.

The father held a soiled piece of wrinkled, often folded and unfolded paper.

This, the father said, is the form.

I thought, the man said, the form was in some arrangement of cartons.

That is what the form explains, the father said, but the form has been corrupted.

The man looked at the form.

The percentages, the man said, are on the sum lines, and the sums are in the percentage boxes. This could be simple reversal.

No, the father said. It must be completed in this way. I check and recheck the entries.

But, the man said, the entries are wrong. Or at least, they are in the wrong places.

Who are you, the father said, to speak of placement?

It is obvious, the man said, from the form.

You do not understand, the father said, how things are placed.

The father walked. The man followed. The father scrutinized the form and mumbled.

The man said nothing.

They came to a large double-door.

Behind this, the father said, what is placed?

The cartons, the man said.

Cartons? The father said. There are not any cartons here. These doors are sealed. Do you understand that?

I believe I do, the man said.

I believe you do not, the father said. I believe you can not. Beyond this, you can not see.

What is there to see, the man said.

That, the father said, is known only to he who can see.

Can you, the man said.

What is there, the father said, but the blooded spasm of pleasure.

Knowest thou the truth.

IV

That was the end of the tract.

Blooded seemed strong. And not encouraging.

He did not know if he was supposed to tell Mallou what he had learned or make notes or otherwise record anything.

He had not learned anything. This kind of teaching – or parable – whatever it was – always confused him.

Like the slides.

The more he saw the slides, the less the slides made any sense.

They seemed to undercut each other.

Or themselves.

As though the enterprise could not maintain its focus for an internally consistent presentation.

If that was the goal.

Maybe the problem was no one knew what the goal was.

The whole banner thing – he had to do it, and he did not mind doing it – but he feared it would not add up to much – to anything.

What did?

World of slides and trips and banners.

If that was all, all should be enough.

If enough was not enough, what could be enough? Ever?

He did not want to ask pointless questions or do pointless things or to be, ultimately, a pointless person.

This was he thought the wrong way to think.

But the tract had not helped.

And the banner.

Whatever banner coming.

Or whichever.

He saw Mallou out in the parking lot.

He was in his room.

Mallou was talking to a man in a suit. Mallou and the man got in a black vehicle and drove off.

He waited. No one told him to.

No one told him not to.

He was raised, as his father before him, in the past, before his own time, preparing for death.

He did not know if he was unique in this or in this perception.

It was not something he thought about.

It was not something that often came up.

Not in the day to day which occupied his days.

In the day to day he trained, as apparently Goerske had, in the Higher Stupidities.

Could he not — was there not still some way — to make Goerske the dog in this thing?

Goerske, who sang:

The Whiskey Gin did a damn fine job /

The Whiskey Gin made me laugh and sob /

The Whiskey Gin showed me some of God /

Or I wrong, I wrong, I wronged.

No wonder nothing worked with the Goerskes of the land running everything.

If he asked, when he had still bothered to ask, he'd get, We're fabrication; you want design.

Or something similar.
Every banner a banner of evasion.
A weight to the meaninglessness of it all.
Grief, maybe, in every banner.
Or series of wrong addresses.
Addressed in misinformation to misinform the ill-informed.
Like the dead man's house of debris visible, or visible now, perhaps always so, shaped now by his previous presence.
Previous presence likely only visible after. Before merely the every day in its presence.
As he saw or thought he saw Mallou everywhere – on the street, in the cheap cafes where he ate, at every noticed displayed banner. Whether it was Mallou, he did not know. Maybe. Maybe somebody who looked like or reminded him of Mallou. Maybe pure illusion.
Element of relief in death in its pure certainty, as in every death, as there would be, he was certain, in his.
No less complicated than the rest of life.
And why might it be.
Expectation.
Which usually revealed the failure of expectation.
Banner went down and was replaced. As though that were the natural order.
Goerske last in line of conformity and its stupid embrace.
Seemed natural order as well.
Hard to see the whole in there somewhere.
Maybe a picture.

Maybe on a banner.

For whales and whatever whales now represent.

Tried to remind himself he was to review banner and banner production for the monograph study.

Necessary, it seemed, to return to first things.

First?

Would Goerske agree to the usage?

Goerske, who had condemned his shirt once in a meeting. He'd appointed the wrong or wronged – it was not clear – shirt, some failure of garment significance or appropriateness.

And Mallou left him brochured.

Brochured and advised.

Advised he needed to revisit the past when he had clearly stated he had neither desire nor inclination to revisit the past.

And then Mallou gone without notice of when Mallou would return.

And then that phantom Mallou he saw everywhere.

Ghost Mallou.

As though the water took him.

Or earth.

Or air.

Or fire.

No sympathy offered him, he offered none to Mallou who was, most likely, alive and living in negligence which was nothing but another word for absence.

If Goerske could send him out here, couldn't Goerske control, or at least direct, Mallou?

Not that he'd go to Goerske with some sad story

after it had been Goerske who had said – who always repeated – in the business of what people can understand, it's all a story.

Bland maxim had its day.

Even, apparently, in the world of banners.

He would not dispute – not with Goerske, not with Mallou – the nature of narrative or the role of image in relation to it.

Survival more and more seemed enough.

Survival better not contemplated and barely noticed.

No banner screened.

Or requested.

Or required.

Though he had once proposed a multiple banner. Multi-paneled, he'd called it. Thought maybe he'd coined something.

Three parts, he thought.

Triptych banner was the idea.

It went nowhere.

Goerske could not shoot it down quickly enough.

And he left to be the sacrifice.

Or take the sacrifice. Recalled some sacrifice in it.

And specter Mallou spectered in Mallou's absence.

He remembered now he had heard of Mallou before he met Mallou.

It was Sirka, back when Sirka was still in the office, who brought up Mallou and said Mallou was indicative of the problem and Goerske was a mere figurehead compared to Mallou and Mallou's pernicious influence discredited the entire enterprise and reflected a profound embrace of decline as the only future.

Sirka went on for some time growing angrier and angrier as Sirka would until Sirka collapsed in a kind of fit and some medical personnel took Sirka away.

That was the end of Sirka though the event was frequently alluded to as Sirka's Diatribe.

Funny, no one called it the Problem of Mallou.

The fit, he supposed, as the fit seemed to seal everything.

Fat satisfaction in that.

And anyway, fit no option for him.

Had to see it through to the banner, nothing else.

Outrage fat in Sirka, but what good had it done Sirka when no one even knew what had become of Sirka other than Sirka was among the gone.

The diatribe a dead, or at least dying, art.

Or form.

He could go back to the brochure, but he felt there was nothing more there.

It was not like he had to memorize it.

And it offered no answer he could see.

Any answer would have to be explained to him.

Spectral Mallou, personally, the explainer.

Should Mallou make Mallou manifest.

Or when.

Knowest thou the truth seemed familiar but as some marketing campaign.

For what he could not recall.

As with the woman who signed her communications S. Forgot whether S was for Sweet or Sweet sally or Sally Sweet or sweetie.

She had had, he believed, a program of some kind.

Then the Holy Ghost got stripped of his title – could happen to anybody – or had.

Or had.

He had no title.

Not really.

So the options for him different or less.

Goerske's afforded contempt, maybe.

Fear on Goerske's part. As though he might declare himself Emperor of the Set Piece and Goerske would be overthrown.

Goerske would go, eventually, but only by fade, as the only way the Goerskes of this world went.

Now for the waiting in the days of rain and what was he to say, the water ran down and frightened me?

Nothing explained.

Nothing, apparently, could be explained.

Nor understood.

All metaphor apt.

The enterprise, he had heard, had obtained 10,000 broken television sets from an arm of the government.

Some surplus sweetheart deal but to what end or possible profit, no one knew.

While they lived, day to day, in brochure.

Maybe the whole thing a loss as part of a tax reduction or evasion scheme.

Maybe some hidden, precious salvage feature.

Value in it.

Watch dog absent.

Some dog that was supposed to bark at a dog.

Goerske had told him to be an artist of happiness.

Goerske empty in Goerske's sarcasm.

He could inform Goerske of the problem of Mallou.

Make Mallou Goerske's problem.

Goerske's specter.

Change things up.

Move things around.

Do some reversal.

Would that be going backwards?

Did that presume he was moving forward?

Backwards to earlier losses, to that legendary loss as the book said.

Goerske would not understand specter anyway.

Only specter was specter imagined.

As he imagined it.

In this darkling life.

Nothing was going to change.

That was what Goerske was saying.

That was, maybe, what Mallou and Mallou's brochure were all about.

A message.

For him.

Triumph against his entire experience, which was nothing, which did not change.

Life as disposition of property.

Death, too, really.

Only blind belief in a benevolent order might save him.

That Mallou's point?
He thought he misunderstood.
Nothing was going to save him.
And no one.
No banner, or few, in that.
Banners for belief aplenty.
For hierarchy as well.
Hierarchy aped hierarchy or the opposite though he saw himself in opposition to no one.
Opposite worse.
Or maybe the same.
As mirror image or mirrored state.
World thick with the dead.
Each made its demands.
What did not?
Even order implied its opposite. Every order.
Or state.
All this slow and cold as life lived in the cold.
Birth cursed nature of the thing – life.
An exhaustion ended not banner celebrated.
Damned to and by the society which damned him – the Goerskes, the Mallous, the rest.
Still, duty to the dead.
Duty of love, maybe.
Still?
And what about Mallou's duty to him?
Should he pepper Mallou with his grocery store demands?
Dead kept coming back, it seemed, while Mallou kept going away.

Ask the dead to stop, maybe.
The dead would not.
The dead beyond the control of the dead.
There was a lion in here somewhere?
Was it a lamb?
Had he not private act severable – away this web of association?
Resort to piety.
Or process.
Or cleverness snide.
Trapped, he knew, in time, culture, class.
Like everyone. Like humans.
Believing something hard desired could be willed into creation.
Or evoked in a banner.
An enforced blindness as self defense. Against the failure of form.
Could form be successful?
Banner castle or castle banner.
Brand of beer, wasn't it?
Everything now sounded like a brand of something else.
Result of branding.
As a banner.
Bit of fabric. Now – more likely plastic – in the wind.
Why other than as thing as any thing?
Precise arrangement precisely delivered.
Or specific.
All a thing was, really.

Defined by its existence.

As everything was or might be understood.

Waiting a debasement in itself. Sent out, and out, restrained before his goal.

Denied.

By Goerske. And likely by Phantom Mallou who seemed little more than Goerske's tool villain.

And was he not complicit in this debasement, in his intent to respect the bannered rites of the dead?

One way to see it.

A way to think of it.

As though he did anything but think.

And wait.

And he but a voice in his own head.

Whatever he had aspired to, surely it was not this.

In service of death abstract which loved him not.

Yet come for him.

After his wait.

After likely years gone in sick and in waste dull and darkening.

A regret.

That he'd have.

He called Goerske to make a demand, but before he could make his demand, Goerske said, You've been misunderstood.

Do you understand, Goerske said.

As though understanding were his intention, and, even if it had been, it was not the understanding Goerske understood as understanding.

He'd have time certain to play that one out.

Who, Goerske said, did you think might orbit this?
That before he could raise Mallou.
Mallou unraised the entire talk.
Not fair to call it conversation.
You are required, Goerske said, to fulfill your requirements.
We'll have, Goerske said, what we have coming from you.
Goerske thought Goerske was at the bottom of it all.
Man at the bottom of it all beneath the ground for that matter and would drive nothing and such again.
Could only he see it?
He was to be finished well before the anniversary.
He could not deny the anniversary.
The anniversary would arrive.
Not like the notebook for projects awaited never to be completed.
Never to be started.
Never to appear or disappear.
Nothing to be made of it.
The anniversary a function of time, of the movement of planets.
The world as the world spun.
Could not be separate from that.
That separate from him.
If he did not finish, Goerske would surely try to finish him.
And Mallou?
He did not know how Mallou would react, but he did not want to work with an angry Mallou.

Not in an industry which was, really, service based.
Lose his retirement.
All linked in estate.
All linked in life.
Whether linkage deserved or not.
Dreamt of the dead man.
Or of a dying friend.
Dream confused jumble of half thought or uncontrolled thought.
Thought to maybe become a crazy man in self defense.
That a surrender.
Whether in compliance or opposition was obscure.
Fathers of the movement once prominent, now forgotten.
What movement?
What fathers?
History as empty as idea, as confused as thought.
Banner an assertion of – an icon for – clarity – if even small clarity.
Clarity of a moment.
Or a place.
A space in place or time.
Frozen in assertion.
And why not?
Why not against chaos?
If chaos it were.

V

Mallou returned.

Not the spectral Mallou or the hallucination.

The actual Mallou returned.

With Mallou was a strange, bearded man who sang several verses of a song that seemed to be called 'Oh, Return not to Me, Boys.'

When the bearded man finished singing, the bearded man left.

He has, Mallou says, a sort of disability or problem. Maybe problems. Who knows?

He asked about the banner plant.

Did you read the brochure?

Yes, he said.

He handed Mallou the brochure.

Mallou leafed through it.

There's a misprint, Mallou said. It's supposed to be 'Bowser Kincaid'. He can talk, not make an addition. Where's the Sword of Fire? The dog doesn't sing. The seal isn't broken. This is not the correct version. It's thoroughly corrupted. Where did this version come from?

You gave it to me, he said. It was the only version – the only version I got.

Well, Mallou said, I can't make head nor tails of this. You know, we've experienced a falling off. I thought there might be a problem with message. This is a problem with message.

It is, he said.

This, Mallou said, is a smoking gun. Let them tell

me it's my imagination now. Let them say no one's responsible. What they mean is no one's accountable. Just because you wear a captain's hat does not make you a captain.

    I'm sure that's correct, he said.

    If you get something wrong, Mallou said, shouldn't you make it right?

    It's a failing, he said.

    It is beginning to fail. Mired in illusion, run until you fall. What else is there? What credible alternative? None, Mallou said. That's what.

    I guess, he said.

    Would you relive the past in the future?

    Is there an alternative?

    This brochure, Mallou said, is part of a protocol. If I get the wrong material, what can I do but pass it on? The agency is supposed to provide the correct materials. That is what the agency is for.

    What agency, he said.

    The agency I work for. The one Goerske hired to train you.

    I'm not in training, he said. I'm working the banner project.

    Banner? You sure you don't want my cousin, the other Mallou? He's big in banners.

    So, he said, what are you giving me, the courtesy tour?

    The agency does training modules. At our office, we can come to you – whatever. It's a revolutionary protocol.

I thought it was a religious tract.

Forgiveness? Love? Something like that? The agency doesn't deliver messages of love.

I don't want to talk about love, he said. My assignment is banners.

A banner signifies something or it shows something or it's pretty or it moves in the wind. You pick out the image from the template – dove for peace, eagle for freedom, sunflower for happiness – like that. Or you design your own. What's a banner but that? Mallou said.

A man could get lost in this, he said. All the dead in their graves and nothing more to it.

How much, Mallou said, does Goerske matter?

Goerske doesn't matter.

Look, Mallou said, I've stood in a bump cap on a catwalk. This agency thing is much better. The dog's silent now. The factory tour isn't a tour. City of magic just looks like a city. Later the dream of the forest evil and the forest good as the book or books foretold.

Is there, he said, a confession in this?

Isn't there? Should there be?

I thought so.

I think not. Maybe you got sent on a boondoggle – you know, get you out and away.

That doesn't say much, he said, for the tribute I was to oversee.

What, Mallou said, are you trying to find?

This. Grief. Everything.

In image imposed on fabric? That seems unlikely.

As unlikely, he said, as anything. As unlikely tribute isn't perfunctory done without marker or icon.

Done for done, Mallou said, leaves you where?

Shuffled in a shuffle, he said. In the middle of the middle. Always there, until end.

Veronica Scott Esposito

Attention & the Future of Narrative

I

Yes – oh, dear, yes – the novel tells a story. That is the fundamental aspect without which it could not exist.

E.M. Forster

A twenty-four-hour movie, looped to be one infinite entertainment, precisely as absorbing as such a foolhardy enterprise would demand.

In 2010, the mixed media artist Christian Marclay finished *The Clock*, a video installation consisting of a timepiece built from film fragments. *The Clock* tells time by appropriating from the vast archive of film history a shot of a clock and/or some other indication of the time of day for every single minute – the rest of the movie's duration being filled in by cinematic bits and pieces. It is typically screened in parallel with the actual time of day, so that *The Clock* is not only an entertainment but also a functional clock.

I was able to watch approximately three hours of *The Clock* at the San Francisco Museum of Modern Art in the spring of 2013, and I've never experienced another narrative quite so absorbing. By the end I was still as fresh and attentive as ever. In fact, I only quit watching as the museum was closing. To this day I am curious to know just how long I would have to watch *The Clock* to become bored with it. Racking my brain for peak artistic encounters of the past twenty-five years, there are very, very few times I can recall where my attention was still so engaged after such a long experience of the same work. Possible equivalents might include the Houston afternoon I spent in the Rothko Chapel; the evening many years ago when I careened through the last two hundred pages of David Foster Wallace's *Infinite Jest*; the time I spent trying to absorb precisely what I was seeing at Teotihuacán in central Mexico; the hour or so in which I stared out across the endless sands after struggling to the top of the great Kelso Sand Dunes in the Mojave Desert.

I have spent a lot of time thinking about why I found *The Clock* so absorbing. Part of it is that the appearance of a new shot every sixty seconds or so provides a strong regularity to the rhythm of its story. Paradoxically, my continual awareness of the time of day made duration fall away from consciousness; often I would find myself losing track of time in the very process of staring at a clock! There is something profoundly lulling about passively receiving a piece of pertinent data – a little bit of feedback – in the course of an entertainment (the modus operandi, of course, of the mobile Internet). These small, predictable bits of feedback that structure *The Clock* are the halo of white noise that enables us to give greater focus to the fascinating things happening on the level of plot in the fifty-five seconds or so out of any given minute that are not occupied with shots of the time of day.

The Clock has no continuous narrative in the conventional sense; rather, its 'plot' is essentially that of a story made entirely out of the middle bits of story: story shorn of its commitments to development, climax, character; story that communicates purely on the level of image, motif, anecdote, aphorism, remark, quip, gesture, expression. Marclay reveals the immense debts he owes to audience conditioning; *The Clock* only works so well because it is able to leverage the years of cinema that its audience has already watched. The innumerable bits of film that constitute the fabric of *The Clock* have the capacity to be effortlessly compelling because they are so immediately recognizable. Even if we have not seen the exact film that Marclay appropriates, we will have seen a film like it, we will know how movies work and so will be able to key in on what makes any given scene entertaining. This is precisely what happens when, flipping through channels late at night, we stop on a film midway through and begin picking up the pertinent details of plot and character, despite having missed all of the exposition and rising action of the story.

The pleasure of *The Clock* is how it serves up this small, effortless challenge again and again – how we implicitly understand that its very form requires it to give us only small fillips of entertainment that are just challenging enough to activate our brains, but not so difficult as to tax our system. Marclay's genius lies in recognizing that plot need not add up to anything at all, so long as each segment of plot is individually compelling on its own and flows seamlessly into the next. This perpetual movement through the middle of narratives is the logic of *The Clock*. It is also the logic of a generation that grew up exposed to information technologies. It is the logic of music videos, which never linger on any particular take long enough for boredom to set in, and whose subjects are always in tantalizing motion, just on the verge of completing some action or revealing something of value. The social media feed displays a similar logic, where one is given an endless stream of bite-sized informational nuggets, which in turn build toward the infinity of content gently force-fed to us through YouTube's autoplay feature. Smaller entertainments such as these culminate in the longer rhythms of a Netflix programming binge, where we are made to consume endless twenty-three-minute chunks of middle plot, technologically engineered to be precisely entertaining enough to keep us watching the next one. Even the basement-entrepreneur filming herself on her smartphone might create an addictive audiovisual experience.

Such entertainments aim to capture what scholars have termed our 'passive' attention – automatic attention that requires little effort to sustain. In this context it is possible to quickly and easily reach a sort of apex of passive attention, the experience known as 'flow', in which there is an ideal balance between effort and resistance – not so easy as to bore you, but not hard enough to make you change tasks.

Literature is different. Literary fiction generally does not work on rhythms short enough to allow such a succession of fixating moments, and cannot take advantage of the self-propulsion and instant identification inherent to moving images. On the contrary, literature is slow. Even the most crowd-pleasing novel typically requires an upfront investment, those fifty or so pages in which one is 'getting into' a story before it is possible to succumb to the charms of plot, the logic of a new and unknown way of seeing the world. In these hours, fiction engages what researchers term our 'active' attention, a kind of attention that requires a much greater deal of mental energy and that is much easier to break – by, say, the chiming of a smartphone or the sudden recollection that one needs to do the laundry.

Of course, there are literary narratives that eventually move into the range of passive attention, the so-called page-turners that can tie down a reader with the grip of fascination, the lure of a secret, the desire to see a villain get come-uppance. This is what keeps the classic triangle-shaped plot described by Gustav Freytag so steady: exposition – rising action – *climax* – falling action – denouement.

Modern novels are often deemed more 'difficult' than traditional novels because they go out of their way to complicate this scheme. If they retain the typical triangular plot structure, they shuffle the chronology so profoundly, or play such bizarre games with point of view, that the traditional pleasures of plot are all but invisible. William Gaddis's infamously difficult *J R* tells the catchy, satirically hilarious story of an 11-year-old boy who parlays his meager stock holdings into becoming a paper tycoon – yet that story is told entirely in unattributed dialogue that jumps so wildly throughout that it becomes 'a blizzard of noise'.

Though they are quite distant from the traditional novel, narratives such as *J R* still bear a trace of Freytag's triangle – indeed, they may be read as conscious efforts to deconstruct it. There are, however, fictions that depart from the triangle altogether. Taking advantage of the discovery of the Freudian unconscious and

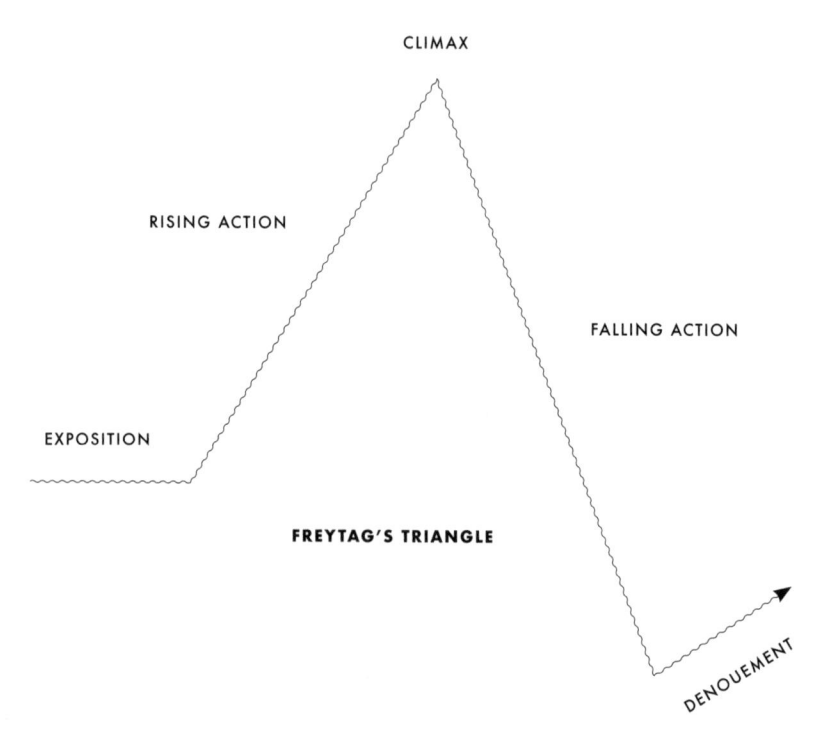

CLIMAX

RISING ACTION

FALLING ACTION

EXPOSITION

FREYTAG'S TRIANGLE

DENOUEMENT

quantum physics, as well as new narrative theories, they have marginalized traditional plotting in favour of exploring new forms that stories might take. What passes for their plot is formed from components that could hardly be described by words like 'beginning', 'middle' and 'end', and, in reality, the experience of such books is less that of a plot than of a series of what we might call conversions.

Like Gerald Murnane, pioneering writers might work with imagistic fragments whose links are unclear. They may, like Ann Quin, sharply blend up time and perspective and style, or, like Gertrude Stein, they may fixate so deeply on language, sound and expression that these concerns swallow up conventions of character and plot. Perhaps, like Borges, they do not tell stories so much as use fictional surfaces to unravel the implications of certain philosophical positions; or, like Enrique Vila-Matas, they pursue anti-narratives that come about through literary criticism and digression. They might, as does Eric Chevillard, prize absolute linguistic originality over logical sense. Like Virginia Woolf, they might depict consciousness in original and initially confusing ways, or, like Beckett, abandon all attempts to represent an interior mind, giving us characters that seem bizarre, unpredictable, inexplicable.

It is no surprise that the works that push the narrative form forward are those that require the greatest amount of sustained focus to assimilate. When an author departs as far as say, Beckett, from the conventions of storytelling, the form of attention necessary to read their work is profoundly altered. We are now squarely in the realm of active attention. While it is quite possible to feel the seamlessness of flow with Beckett or Woolf, this typically happens when we are re-reading their work, or after we have read so much of it that we already have a firm grasp of how it functions.

This is a profoundly different condition from the absorption that carried me through three hours of Marclay's *The Clock*, which builds its fascination out of pieces that are absolutely familiar to anybody living in the developed world, and which relies on well-disseminated conventions to attract and sustain attention. *The Clock* dips into the great middle hump of the normal curve, whereas Beckett and Woolf ask me to venture out into the sliver-thin fringes at its long tail. If *The Clock* throws us into a world where one familiar thing leads to another, then another, then another, then Beckett and Woolf put us in a space where one thing *becomes* another, *becomes* another, *becomes* another: a progression of transformations in which we must constantly rediscover our position. With the former it is simple to say why certain events follow each other – the plot conventions that we have absorbed every single day of our lives explain it. But the ways in which we explain the latter – with its recondite, metaphorical, highly idiosyncratic conversions – are more doubtful. Lacking such ready-made causation, the matter of narrative becomes obscure.

It is my belief that the further we get from Freytag's triangle the closer we draw to the kind of distilled, purely literary attention that can only come from sustained works of prose. The further we get from plot, and the more we tread toward language's pure representation of experience, the closer we come to seeing precisely what literary fiction can do.

Fiction holds no monopoly on plot. E.M. Forster is undoubtedly correct that plot is the common denominator to all works of fiction, but it is equally true that plot is not unique to literature, and, what's more, at this point in time prose is surely not the storytelling medium whose plots elicit attention most successfully. Plot only exists in fiction as a basic requirement of the genre, not because anyone consciously chooses to put it there. It is like the water that composes over seventy percent of our brain – necessary, preponderant, beside the point.

> Yes – oh, dear, yes – the novel tells a story. That is the fundamental aspect without which it could not exist. That is the highest factor common to all novels, and I wish that it was not so, that it could be something different – melody, or perception of the truth, not this low atavistic form.
> (E.M. Forster, *Aspects of the Novel*)

Forster rightly calls storytelling 'atavistic' – it is archaic, likely the oldest artistic practice known to humanity, something without which language as we know it would be inconceivable. But twentieth-century fiction is quite new. It is a radically new form of literary expression congruent with the equally radical conditions of abundance, urbanism, hyper-globalization, late capitalism, and electronic mass media that emerged alongside it. These idiosyncratic fictions maintain the requirements of story in a vestigial sense, but story as conceived and popularized in the heyday of the novel is far from their primary concern, and so they lose the more universal appeal of familiarity and instead rely on the audience's having the correct education and predispositions. Cultural context here is key, as are social sphere, school of thought, intellectual predilection, educational background, quantity of patience ... they are all now essential in maintaining the proper working order of the machinery of attention. This is what is meant when a writer is called 'difficult'. But here is the novel's unique contribution to human thought: the capacity to showcase varieties of experience that have never achieved representation elsewhere, and pioneer methods of relating two or more different phenomena in entirely unforeseen ways.

Though they can appear similar, there is a difference between nonsense and extreme singularity of vision, between an observation that is purely banal and one subtle enough to open an entirely new system of thought. In the latter case, there is always a hidden structure, a submerged iceberg of knowledge or insight. In diving beneath the surface, attention does not only receive the next link in the chain of causation, the mind is enkindled by the possibility of discovering forms that defy the architecture of thought. The mind is fired by geometries that require it to leap beyond its current capacities, that push beyond what the human mind can currently do.

Furthest of all from Freytag's triangle is a kind of fiction that relentlessly resists systemization, that is constantly rediscovering its center – fiction, it might be claimed, that tells stories as poetry. *Montano's Malady* by Enrique Vila-Matas, Kazuo Ishiguro's *The Unconsoled*, Gerald Murnane's *Border Districts* exhibit this continual re-centering to a greater or lesser degree. Éric Chevillard's absurdist, abundant *Palafox* pushes plot to a singularly dynamic place. Literature that focuses its energies on things other than story ultimately proves the absolute truth of Forster's observation, that story will find its way into every fiction, even those that entirely disregard it.

II

I don't want something already made but something still being tortuously made.

Clarice Lispector

But let us leave literature and turn again to the digital tumult. The novel has long feared its obsolescence, if not necessarily its exhaustion (how could one ever exhaust this form that swallows all other forms?), and nowadays these fears are most commonly projected towards digital media. The novel itself was once the attention-grabbing emergent medium, itself riding a wave of mass dissemination unparalleled in Western history. This history is buried in its DNA, and it knows, deep down, that nothing else will ever perform quite as it can.

What, then, are the differences between the experience of print and digital? In the literary sphere we grapple with one mind at a time; in the digital sphere there is always a mass of other minds. If all forms of reading might be imagined as variations on the simple act of driving down a road, then reading a novel might be like driving down a lonely, very long, very straight one-lane desert road in the isolation of a perfectly soundless night, whereas reading online is like being on an eight-lane, twisting superhighway full of bumper-to-bumper traffic consisting of drivers all honking uproariously at you while in your car shriek innumerable cell phones all calling for you and four unruly passengers scream at your face.

The online world may be chaotic, but the purpose of this anarchy of attention-seeking is not anarchic. For, once an entertainment has managed to seize a Web consumer's attention, its purpose is to maintain that attention as long as possible by means of a lulling, endless stream of feedback and middle-narrative, in the manner of *The Clock*. Marclay's creation is not just a mega-instance of televisual/cinematic culture, a consolidation of the entire history of modern mass visual culture into one totalizing, era-capping supercut, it is also a handing of the attention-seeking baton to the Internet, a forward-looking piece that intuitively understands a staggering amount about what makes twenty-first-century media so addictive.

Any storytelling medium requires an upfront investment of active attention before we slip into passivity. But with each new innovation in electronic culture that upfront investment decreases, to the point where a piece like Marclay's *The Clock* requires almost none at all.

The novel provides the reader with a self-contained, singular narrative experience. The digital realm confronts us with the raw flow of many narratives, all constantly impinging on each other. What can one do from within this headlong gush but join in? Whispering, subtlety and complexity are for those who confidently claim the privilege of deep focus, trusting in an audience that will patiently apply active attention for dozens of hours. In the sphere of constant electronic content, the rule is the *thonk!*, the familiar and the clear, and the endless anxiety of losing audience share to something newer, faster, louder and more pandering.

The online space is an endless competition for passive attention, a limitless caterwauling of catering to expectations. Here survival of the fittest rules. Like an intrepid species that survives one existential challenge after another, the best citizens of the digital sphere are constantly self-shaping, changing their very DNA with every click, always updating their code and algorithms to better maintain their grip on our attention. This is in fact the exact mission of many of the best-educated, wealthiest, most empowered individuals who have ever lived on this planet, people who now command thousands of engineers making use of the most advanced technology ever manufactured. Day by day, week by week, their goal is to make the digital world a more absorbing medium. As life is increasingly experienced through digital mediation – that is, as massive techno-media empires fight harder and more efficiently to package everything we experience on Earth through the Internet – our perception of the world has gradually gravitated toward something resembling Marclay's *Clock*, an all-consuming, never-ending advance through engrossing bits of narrative precisely calibrated to seize our passive attention.

No good. The plot of life is in constant need of difficulty, as much as history is in need of unforeseen innovation. An all-consuming life of pre-ordained, endless, banal plots was the horror of *The Matrix* and *1984*. Such well-plotted lives are inimical to the human spirit, and unchanging histories are corrosive to societies. As people lose the ability to cultivate the unforeseen, they will fall captive to those who have mastered the old stories. They lose their ability to imagine new alternatives for themselves, they will be damned to the familiar failings and debates, their lives will be consumed by old solutions that no more fit their changing world than a baby shoe fits an adult.

Narrative is the principal means by which we comprehend the trajectory of individual lives and the history of our species. We once orally told each other stories to make sense of the world we live in. Later we painstakingly inscribed these tales in manuscript form, then mass-produced them with printing presses and read silently in unprecedented numbers. After that they were dispersed through broadcast culture to even wider audiences, and now, as the Internet has begun to take its share of the storytelling pie, the personal computer, that object without which modern life would be unthinkable, his becoming the locus of our personal and historic narratives. Facebook in 2017 claimed two billion active users worldwide – just over one-quarter of all humanity; to this we might add the nearly one billion users of WeChat, the closest existing approximation to Facebook in China, where that website is blocked. This would bring us to over one-third of all people on Earth using this medium to chronicle their lives and witness the narratives of their friends and other nations.

Millennials have been estimated to check their phones over 150 times per day. Studies have concluded that social media occupies two hours of the average adult day (an amount that is still behind daily television use, but only just). Smartphone usage is estimated at four hours per day. As print culture has given way to broadcast media and now the Internet, mass attention has drifted from fully formed Freytag-like narratives toward the endless drip-drip-drip of discrete, minute narrative points. At this point, the fragmentation is more complete than ever.

And the construction of dominant narratives in the online space is decided increasingly by non-human actors. Data regarding various types of views and clicks has thoroughly quantified attention for use by mathematical algorithms, while the ease and rapidity of electronic networks has potentiated the effects of community and market forces, stripping away human agency. As we have seen in recent electoral cycles, this system has allowed the establishment of narratives that do not have any basis in reality and whose authors and beneficiaries are difficult to discern. The logic of these Web-based narratives has begun to reverse-colonize literature, film and TV, at times under the guise of innovation. In the literary sphere there is now a proliferation of fragmentary novels, autofictions and lyric essays, many of which anticipated the online space, and many of which are of quite high literary quality, but which by and large are not now innovating on the level necessary to create new ways of seeing the world that are significantly divorced from the online point of view.

Technology's influence is clear; it is incumbent upon the printed form not to sway with its dictates. If mass electronic media will decide the terms of the contemporary competition for attention, fiction will have to make its own stand in its own way.

III

My experience is what I agree to pay attention to.
William James

The human body is a vessel for perception. All the knowledge produced throughout the entire history of the human species comes solely from our experience of the world. Quite fundamentally, from our attention comes our version of reality.

As William James rightly observed, that which is most familiar to us is most able to lay claim to our attention. There is no reason why life should follow a path that is chiefly – or solely – concerned with those things most amenable to our attention; such a life is one of insularity and circularity, a life of dullness that we would not even able to recognize as such.

Literature is our foremost means of encountering existential connections to the unforeseen. Perhaps now that other media have so handily exceeded the novel's once formidable capacities to construct engrossing stories and garner passive attention, it is today easier than ever to see the novel's strengths in pushing us toward new experiences of the world. It is still an unequaled form for developing ideas to their very limit, a practice that is perhaps undervalued in an imagistic culture fixated on speed and novelty, and put off by slowness and the patience required by truly original argumentation.

What are the contemporary conceptual counterparts to quantum physics, Freudian psychology, Marxism, fascism, post-industrialized democracy? What new forms do they encourage the novelist to investigate, and how will these forms push those concepts beyond the threshold of our understanding and into new knowledge? How will the literature of the twenty-first century counteract the technological systems that are quickly forging dominant identities, just as twentieth-century literature broke down the systems of its day? Where will this literature find agency in a world more and more crowded with ideology, fashion and automation? Where will it locate humanity in a story increasingly run by, through and for machines?

As ever, we must have writers capable of creating varieties of experience whose singularity compels our attention, and readers who are worthy of them.

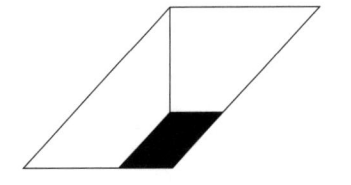

Sponsors

AVAILABLE NOW FROM FUTURE TENSE BOOKS

futuretensebooks.com

I Don't Think of You (Until I Do) by Tatiana Ryckman

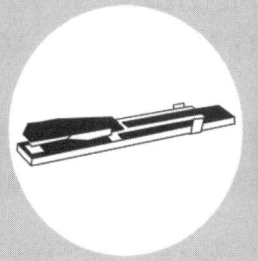

Assisted Living by Gary Lutz

Coming Summer '18: *Pretend We Live Here* by Genevieve Hudson

---

CALAMARI NOW

is based in Rome + publishes uncopyrighted anonymous or pseudonymous books (+ music cassettes). **In the past** 15 years, Calamari Archive has published 70 book objects (including *Sleepingfish* magazine + the acquired *3rd bed* imprint). Some of these have been first books by emerging writers such as Blake Butler, Miranda Mellis, Robert Lopez, Peter Markus + Chiara Barzini, while others have been resurrected reprints of out-of-print cult classics by established writers such as David Ohle, Stanley Crawford, Gary Lutz + Scott Bradfield.

CALAMARI ARCHIVE, INK.

www.calamaripress.com

■▮ TEST CENTRE
INDEPENDENT PUBLISHER OF THE SPOKEN AND WRITTEN WORD

POETRY | FICTION | ANTHOLOGIES
MAGAZINES | VINYL

RECENT TITLES:

Test Centre Eight
ft. David Hayden, Oli Hazzard, Jen Calleja, Iain Sinclair, Kathryn Maris, Stephen Watts & many more

The Magic Door by Chris Torrance

lemon, egg, bread by Laura Elliott

Nights of Poor Sleep by Rachael Allen & Marie Jacotey

Safe Mode by Sam Riviere

Currently & Emotion: Translations, ed. Sophie Collins

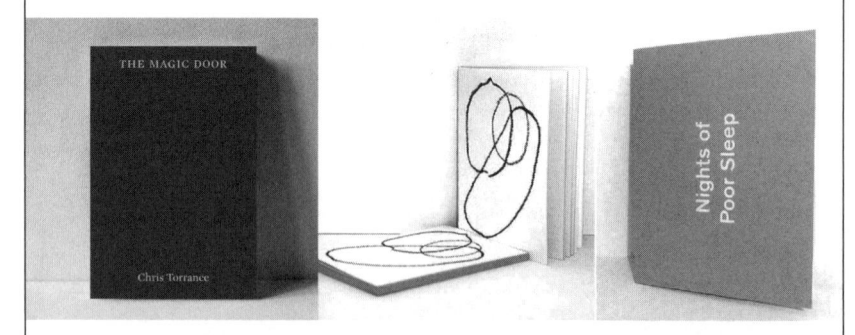

"Test Centre have returned Hackney to a state of readiness and experimental action." – Iain Sinclair

www.testcentre.org.uk | @TestCentre77

'*Pure Hollywood* is pure gold. Come for the art of her exquisitely weird writing and stay for the human drama.'
Ottessa Moshfegh

PRAISE FOR CHRISTINE SCHUTT

'Pared down but rich, dense, fevered, exactly right and eerily beautiful.'
John Ashbery

'A truly gifted writer.'
George Saunders

Available for pre-order now and purchase from 10 May 2018
www.andotherstories.org/book/pure-hollywood

www.andotherstories.org
@andothertweets
andotherstoriesbooks
@andotherpics

And Other Stories

LY SEPPEL
MERRILL MOORE
WILLIAM PLOMER
BINK NOLL
SAVKAR ALTINEL
TIMOTHY OGENE
IAN HOLDING
MICHAEL CUGLIETTA
ROSANNA MCLAUGHLIN
ANDRES EHIN
LOLA RIDGE
RUSSELL PERSSON
JASON SCHWARTZ
DAVID HAYDEN
GORDON LISH
KATHRYN SCANLAN

LITTLE ISLAND PRESS

The Stinging Fly

New writers, new writing since 1998

Two print issues per year

Subscribers receive free access to our complete online archive

www.stingingfly.org @stingingfly

DARKER WITH THE LIGHTS ON
by David Hayden

"Here is language to live in. David Hayden is a serious force."
SAM LIPSYTE

Out this May in paperback

The Fitzcarraldo Editions Novel Prize is an annual competition rewarding ambitious, imaginative and innovative writing. The winner will receive a £3,000 prize as an advance against publication with Fitzcarraldo Editions. The winning novel will subsequently be published in Fitzcarraldo Editions' fiction list. Submissions are open from 15 April to 15 July 2018. The judges will be looking for novels which explore and expand the possibilities of the form, which are innovative and imaginative in style, which tackle subjects and themes relevant to the world we live in.

For more details please visit fitzcarraldoeditions.com

Fitzcarraldo Editions

TRANSIT BOOKS

SUCH SMALL HANDS
ANDRÉS BARBA
Translated by LISA DILLMAN
With an afterword by EDMUND WHITE

KINTU

Swallowing Mercury
Longlisted The Man Booker International Prize 2017
Wioletta Greg

LESSONS for a CHILD who arrives LATE
TRANSLATED BY VALERIE MILES
Carlos Yushimito

OAKLAND, CALIFORNIA
transitbooks.org

'STRANGE, ENIGMATIC AND FULL OF MAGIC.'
— Maggie Nelson

'Forget whatever you previously associated with "fairy tales," and enter Carol Mavor's kaleidoscopic universe of art and literature. Everyone from Ralph Eugene Meatyard to Kiki Smith to Frank Baum to Emmett Till to Francesca Woodman to Langston Hughes is here, and so many more, held together by Mavor's casually erudite, finely spun web.'

— Maggie Nelson

OUT NOW IN HARDBACK

Available to order from
www.reaktionbooks.co.uk
and other bookshops.

Aurelia
ART AND LITERATURE THROUGH THE MOUTH OF THE FAIRY TALE
CAROL MAVOR

312 pages | RRP. £25

www.reaktionbooks.co.uk
@ReaktionBooks

*award-winning and shortlisted poetry collections
from*

CARCANET

SINÉAD MORRISSEY On Balance

*winner of the Forward Prize for Poetry (Best Collection)
shortlisted for the Costa Book Awards*

CAROLINE BIRD In These Days of Prohibition
ROBERT MINHINNICK Diary of the Last Man
TARA BERGIN The Tragic Death of Eleanor Marx

shortlisted for the T.S. Eliot Prize

---

available at carcanet.co.uk and in all good book shops

In the first issue: Jen Calleja, Rishi Dastidar, Will Eaves, Inua Ellams, Sophie Herxheimer, Angelina D'Roza

BRIXTON REVIEW OF BOOKS

A new literary quarterly, freely distributed around South London; or available on subscription via www.brixtonreviewofbooks.net

---

EGRESS
NEW OPENINGS IN LITERARY ART

To advertise in forthcoming issues, please contact the editors at:

egress@littleislandpress.co.uk

Contributors

Eley Williams is writer-in-residence at the University of Greenwich. Publications include *Frit* and *Attrib. and Other Stories*.

David Hayden was born in Dublin. His book of stories, *Darker with the Lights On*, is published by Little Island Press in the UK and in North America by Transit Books.

Evan Lavender-Smith is the author of *From Old Notebooks* and *Avatar*. He is an assistant professor of English at Virginia Tech. Learn more at www.el-s.net.

Kathryn Scanlan's work has appeared in *NOON*, *Fence* and *American Short Fiction*. Her debut book of stories, *The Dominant Animal*, will be published by Little Island Press in the UK in 2018 and FSG in the US in 2019.

Kimberly King Parsons is the author of *Black Light*, a collection of short stories forthcoming from Vintage in 2019. She lives in Portland, OR.

Veronica Scott Esposito is the author of four books, including *The Doubles* and *The Surrender*. Her writing has appeared in *The New York Times*, the *Times Literary Supplement* and many others.

Kevin McMahon is a motion picture story analyst and father of two.

Greg Mulcahy is the author of *Out of Work, Constellation, Carbine* and *O'Hearn*. He lives in Minnesota.

Sam Lipsyte is the author of *The Ask* and *The Fun Parts*, among other books. *Hark*, a novel, will appear in early 2019.

Brian Evenson is the author of over a dozen books of fiction, most recently *A Collapse of Horses*. He lives and works in Los Angeles.

Diane Williams is the author of eight books of fiction and the editor of *NOON*. Her *Collected Stories* is due out from Soho Press in October.

Lily Hackett is a writer based in Cambridge, UK, working freelance for a number of publications including *Noises Off* and *Dazed & Confused*. She is currently writing a series of stories about food and dining.

Christine Schutt is the author of three novels and three story collections, the most recent, *Pure Hollywood*. Schutt has been a finalist for the National Book Award and Pulitzer Prize.

Laura Ellen Joyce has written *The Museum of Atheism, The Luminol Reels, Luminol Theory* and *The Locus Terribilis in Contemporary Crime Drama*.

Gordon Lish wears brown. He used to wear grey. When still subject to the taste of his elders, he wore, or was dressed in, blue, of which experience he has no memory. The substance of the foregoing admissions have had no little to do with what he has done to bear his person in his costume into the maiden issue of *Egress*.

Carrie Cooperider is a writer and visual artist living in New York City.

Grant Maierhofer is the author of, most recently, *Clog*, out in July 2018 from Inside the Castle.

EGRESS welcomes submissions, including from previously unpublished writers. No cover letter is necessary.

www.littleislandpress.co.uk/egress